I0744648

Also by Peg Tittle

(fiction)

Gender Fraud: a fiction (forthcoming)
Impact (forthcoming)
Exile
What Happened to Tom

(nonfiction)

Just Think About It
Sexist Shit that Pisses Me Off
No End to the Shit that Pisses Me Off
Still More Shit that Pisses Me Off
More Shit that Pisses Me Off
Shit that Pisses Me Off

Ethical Issues in Business:
Inquiries, Cases, and Readings (2nd ed.)
Critical Thinking: An Appeal to Reason
What If … Collected Thought Experiments in Philosophy
Should Parents be Licensed? Debating the Issues

It Wasn't Enough

It Wasn't Enough

Peg Tittle

Magenta

It Wasn't Enough
© 2015 by Peg Tittle

pegtittle.com

First published 2020

978-1-926891-71-2 (print)
978-1-926891-72-9 (pdf)
978-1-926891-73-6 (epub)

Published by Magenta

This is a work of fiction. Names, characters, places, brands, media, and incidents are either the product of the author's imagination or are used fictitiously. The author acknowledges the trademarked status and trademark owners of various products referenced in this work of fiction, which have been used without permission. The publication/use of these trademarks is not authorized, associated with, or sponsored by the trademark owners.

Cover design by Elizabeth Beeton and Peg Tittle

Formatting and interior book design by Elizabeth Beeton

Library and Archives Canada Cataloguing in Publication

Title: It wasn't enough / Peg Tittle.
Other titles: It was not enough
Names: Tittle, Peg, 1957- author.
Identifiers: Canadiana (print) 20200160869 | Canadiana (ebook) 20200160877 | ISBN 9781926891712
   (softcover) | ISBN 9781926891729 (PDF) | ISBN 9781926891736 (EPUB)
Classification: LCC PS8639.I76 I89 2020 | DDC C813/.6—dc23

Thanks to...

Mar Iguana—she put the premise/idea into my head (via her post on feministcurrent.com)

Catia Luong, Hailey Boutin, Ben Gorman, and especially Callie Yaeger

Pete Karageorgos, Insurance Bureau of Canada

Noel Bennett, Peterborough Regional Health Center

Wil Wheaton for his tweet regarding male gamer responses to Anita Sarkeesian

This is a work of fiction, but it is based on facts;
see the list of references at the end of the novel.

One day, the women were gone.

It was … an opportunity.

1

Timmy's crying woke him up. Or maybe it was Tommy's crying. Diane could always tell which one it was, but he never could. Even though there were two years between them.

"Diane!" he called out to her. With annoyance. She must already be up, he thought, because she wasn't in the bed beside him. Though, since they'd had an argument the night before—correction, another argument—that didn't surprise him. She was spending more nights in the boys' room these days. He'd told her that's why she couldn't leave. Because of the boys. He hadn't meant it to come out like they were holding her hostage. But it did. He sometimes wondered if that's why he'd pushed her to have kids. To make sure she didn't leave. Because, truthfully, he didn't really—oh he loved them, of course, they were his kids, but …

"Diane!" he called out again, more loudly. The other one had started crying as well.

"Mommy …"

"Mom*my!*"

He groaned, then got up. It was time anyway. He glanced at the clock on the night table. Shit! Past time! No, no, no, he muttered as he raced to the shower, he couldn't be late today, he was presenting his report to the Board at ten. He'd been working on it all week … Diane usually woke him—where the hell was she?

On his way to the bathroom, he saw that she wasn't in the boys' room. Timmy and Tommy were there, wailing away, but Diane was nowhere to be seen.

"Diane!" he yelled. Damn it! He went into the room, picked Timmy up out of his crib, and started jostling him, trying to make him stop crying.

"Shh, it's okay, Daddy's here …"

"Where's Mommy?" Tommy whined. "I want *Mommy!*"

He carried Timmy out with him, Tommy close on his heels, glanced in the bathroom, then went downstairs. No Diane. Had she left after all? She would've gone to her parents' place. He didn't see a note, but he was sure there would be one. A long, scathing analysis of each of his many faults. A protracted description about how she was unhappy, unfulfilled, and—

At the moment, he had more pressing concerns. *He'd* have to get the boys ready and take them to daycare.

He returned to the boys' room, and started to—truthfully, he didn't know their routine. He changed Timmy's diaper. He helped Tommy go potty. He dressed them. He fed them. He dressed them again. It was all very difficult. Apparently he wasn't doing anything right.

"Juice!" Timmy had insisted.

"Okay, here you go," Andrew poured some juice into Timmy's sippy cup and gave it to him. Timmy threw the cup onto the floor, and the juice seeped out.

"Timmy!" He yelled at him then reached for a tea towel to wipe it up. Timmy started crying. Again.

"Sorry, Daddy's sorry," he said, taking a cursory swipe at the spill, then lifting him out of his chair. Where the *hell* was Diane?

"Why isn't Mommy here?" Tommy asked.

"I don't know."

"Why?"

Andrew ignored him.

"When's Mommy coming home?" Tommy tried a different approach. And then, for good measure, wandered over to the stove.

"I don't know, Tommy. Please sit and eat your cereal," Andrew said. He'd put Timmy back in his chair and was wrestling with the coffee maker.

"Don't want to." He ran his little fingers over the knobs. Andrew pulled him away and forced him into his chair. How was he supposed to take a shower let alone make a cup of coffee? He couldn't turn his back on them for a minute …

"Eat!" He'd had enough. It was eight-thirty already.

"No!" Tommy threw his spoon onto the floor. And then his bowl of cereal.

By nine o'clock, Andrew was finally ready to leave the apartment. He'd managed a two-minute shower, but not a shave. And not a cup of coffee. He put Timmy into the stroller, grabbed his laptop case, then went out the door to the elevator, making sure that Tommy was following. He bumped the door in his rush, and Timmy started crying again. Down the hallway, into the elevator— no, Tommy refused to get in. He seemed to have developed a fear of elevators that Andrew knew nothing about. So Andrew pushed the button to keep the doors open, set his laptop case onto the elevator floor beside the stroller, then went back out to pick him up.

At the parking lot level, he managed to push the stroller out of the elevator without setting Tommy down. As soon as the doors closed, he realized he'd forgotten his laptop. Shit! He pressed the button immediately, but someone else must've beaten him to it. He waited anxiously, watching the floor indicators light up as the elevator ascended, stopped at the sixth floor, then started re-descending. It stopped again, at the lobby level—damn it, was some good Samaritan taking his laptop to the 'Lost and Found'? Better that than stealing it, but— When the doors opened, he was relieved to see that it was exactly where he'd left it.

After putting the two boys into their car seats—almost a five-minute ordeal—Andrew drove out and into the street.

At the first stoplight, he called Sharon, his assistant, to let her know he was running late. There was no answer.

At the second stoplight, he called her again. Still no answer. Where the hell was she? He called general reception instead. Brittany or Brianna or whatever could get a message to Sharon. Again, no answer. What the hell? Was she too busy sitting there filing her nails? Actually, he thought a little shamefacedly, he'd never seen her sitting there filing her nails … He tossed the phone onto the passenger seat in disgust, then saw it slide off the seat and out of reach. Damn it!

"Where's Mommy?" Tommy asked again.

"I don't know!" Andrew said, again. "She went to Grammy's."

"Why?"

Andrew ignored him. Again.

He was surprised to see some sort of traffic jam in the daycare parking lot. Since he was so late, he'd expected an empty lot. He figured all the moms would have been there and gone already. But no, the lot was a mess, with cars haphazardly pulled up around the door. And all he saw were dads.

Andrew slapped the steering wheel in frustration as he pulled up behind the part that most looked like a line. He didn't have time for this today! He had An Important Meeting to get to!

He watched with some confusion as men got out of their cars, stomped to the door, kids in tow, only to stomp back to their cars, gesticulating and shouting at other men. After a few minutes, during which the car in front of him hadn't moved at all, hadn't been able to move, Andrew got out to see what the trouble was.

"Fucking bitches musta gone on strike or something!" a man with a huge belly said. It occurred to Andrew, for the first time, to wonder whose kids his kids were playing with every day …

"Hey!" another one said sharply. "I'll thank you for watching your language in front of my three-year old!" He put his arms protectively around a little red-haired boy.

"I'm jus' sayin'—"

"I heard what you were jus' sayin'," the other man mocked, "and I doubt that's true. I doubt the women even know each other."

Was everyone's wife gone? Is that what had happened? Or was the guy just talking about the daycare staff—

"Wouldn't they though?" a bearded man spoke up. "Know each other? I mean, if it's always our wives who drop off our kids ..." he trailed off. A strike didn't seem plausible, but ...

"*My* wife has no reason to go on strike," the watch-your-language man said. Smugly, Andrew thought. And, given that, probably incorrectly.

"Is there *no* one here?" Andrew asked then, walking up to try the door. As if he was the only one with brains enough to have thought to do that.

The door was locked. Of course.

Andrew stood around for another minute, trying to figure it out, but then decided there was no more information to be had, so he went back to his car. He'd have to take the boys to work with him.

He'd never realized until that day that whoever designed revolving doors must not have had kids.

Then, after struggling with yet another elevator, he saw that Sharon wasn't at her desk. Damn it! He'd intended to ask her to get him a cup of coffee.

He started to detour to the small lunch room at the end of the hall, but then realized he couldn't manage the stroller, his laptop case, *and* a cup of coffee.

So first he got the kids settled into his office, more or less. It was quarter to ten.

"Daddy's going to get a cup of coffee," he told Tommy. "Watch your brother, okay? I'll be back in a minute."

As he rushed out and down the hall, ignoring Timmy's wail as he disappeared, he saw Matthew come out of the lunch room, coffee cup in hand. Great!

The coffee pot was empty.

"Hey!" he called after him.

"What?"

"You took the last cup!"

"Your point?"

"You should have started another pot!"

"Not my job," he smiled.

"Well, whose job is it?" Andrew asked. "Who made the cup you have?"

Matthew shrugged.

"I did," Kyle said, coming into the room. "Jackass!" he called after Matthew.

"Listen," Andrew started, "could you make another pot? I've got my kids in my office—"

"Me too," Kyle said curtly as he quickly tossed the used filter into the garbage and reached into the cupboard for another one. "We're going to run out of these before the end of the day," he noted. "Could you take care of that?"

"Okay," Andrew had to say, as he watched Kyle measure coffee into the new filter then set it to percolate.

"Thanks," he added, nodding to the gurgling pot. "Ten minutes?"

"Be gone then, come back in five," he said grimly as he left.

Andrew returned to his office, relieved to see the boys still there and out of mischief. More or less. Timmy had stopped crying and was still in his stroller, but he was struggling with the straps. Tommy was spinning around in Andrew's chair.

He lifted Tommy up out of the chair and set him onto the carpeted floor beside Timmy. As an afterthought, he tossed him a pencil and ... a handful of his business cards. He'd find something better later ... "Can you make some pictures? Daddy has to work."

"Why?"

Andrew sat down to take a breath, glancing at his watch. Ten minutes. The meeting started in ten minutes. He opened his laptop and turned it on.

Richard, his boss, sauntered in. "Andrew, my boy ..."

Andrew tensed. He hated when Richard called him that. He was thirty-five for god's sake. And Richard wasn't that much older. Fifty, tops.

"It seems there's some sort of problem with the ladies, and I'm sure it's nothing," he waved his hand dismissively, "but we need you to answer the phones today."

"What?" Andrew looked at him in disbelief. He was a Project Manager. He had a university degree for god's sake. And he wanted him to answer phones? He couldn't be serious.

"But I have the meeting with the Board—"

"Not to worry, I'll take care of that for you, if you'll just give me your report," Richard said smoothly.

And let him take the credit? No way. But Richard was staring at him. Waiting. Apparently he had no choice.

"Okay, I'll just get Sharon to—"

"Sharon's not here. Weren't you listening? None of the women are here."

"What?" Andrew said again. But he'd intended to ask Sharon to look after his kids while he was at the meeting. She'd had kids of her own—no, maybe she hadn't—now that he thought about it, he couldn't remember seeing any pictures on her desk—in any case, she was no Brittany or Brianna, with whom he'd never leave his kids. Sharon was older and far more responsible; in fact, she had been the one who'd trained him when he first came to the company.

"*None* of the women are here?" Andrew stared out the window, trying to make sense of it.

"Your report?" Richard was waiting.

"Oh—"

"Andrew," he said, with *such* exasperation, "what seems to be the problem?"

Seems to be. As if there really wasn't any problem. Did he do that on purpose? My boy. Seems to be.

"Sharon has it. I mean, I have it," he glanced at his laptop, "but she was going to format it and ..." Make it all neat and tidy. She did that with all of his reports.

"We don't have time for that now, just give me what you've got."

Andrew opened the report. He was about to hit 'Print' but ... it looked so ... incompetent.

"Can't we just reschedule?" he asked hopefully.

"No, the Board needs to see the numbers now," Richard said impatiently. "Just print it and I'll be on my way."

Sighing, he pressed 'Print' and they both went to the printer. A dotted triangle was flashing. No report was forthcoming.

"Did you press 'Print'?" Richard asked, patronizingly.

"Yes, I pressed 'Print'!" Andrew said angrily.

"I don't have time for this," Richard said with disgust a moment later, as if the failing printer was Andrew's fault. "Put the report on a flash drive, then get to the phones." They'd been ringing since Richard had shown up. Since before he'd shown up, actually.

Andrew returned to his office and a few moments later reluctantly handed Richard a flash drive.

Richard turned and only then noticed Andrew's kids in the corner.

"What are those?" he asked coldly.

Andrew stared at him. With a look of incomprehension on his face that could only be said to match that on his boss's face.

"Kids," he replied. "My kids, Timothy and Thomas."

"And you brought them here to work with you because ..."

"My wife—"

He waved his hand. Didn't want to hear it.

"Make other arrangements," was all he said. "And get to those phones."

Again, Andrew just stared at him, as he sauntered out. With *his* report.

"And see to the printer, would you?" Richard called back.

If Andrew had had a slammable door, he would've slammed it after Richard. Instead, he simply picked up Timmy, mercifully quiet all this time, and put out his hand for Tommy.

There was no real place for the kids to settle in the reception area. It was open concept, with no corner. It wasn't even carpeted. Andrew went back to his office for the stroller. There was no way Timmy would be content to sit in his stroller for very long, but what alternative did he have? Maybe he'd fall asleep. He lifted Tommy back into his desk chair and pulled it along behind him, awkwardly manoeuvring it around the counter.

Now what? He opened the top drawer of the receptionist's desk, found a couple highlighters, then went to the printer for some blank sheets of paper.

"Can you make some more pictures while Daddy works?" he said to Tommy, thinking to clear a bit of space on the receptionist's desk. But no, that looked impossible. He looked around, then grabbed a clipboard from the counter top, put the blank sheets of paper on top of what looked like a sign-in sheet, and handed it to Tommy.

"All set?"

Tommy nodded. Morosely.

"Will somebody *please* answer those goddamned phones?" Matthew stuck his head out his door as Andrew sat down at the desk.

He picked up the ringing phone.

"Hello?"

He heard nothing. The line was dead. No, it kept ringing. He pushed the flashing red button labelled '1'.

"Hello?"

"Hello— Is this Stride Enterprises?"

"Yes." He'd just noticed that there was a column of such buttons, labelled 1-5. There were five lines? He had to answer five phones?

"May I speak to Mr. Belsen?"

"Um, just a minute."

Andrew looked around for some sort of directory. There, pinned to the fabric of the reception divider right in front of him. When he reached out to run his finger down the list, it fluttered off the divider. Which, he realized, wasn't really made for stuff to be pinned onto. Whose bright idea was that? It should be cork board or something. The list had fluttered between the divider and the desk, onto the floor. Damn it! He had to get onto his hands and knees and crawl under the desk to reach it. Tommy eagerly helped. And got his hands covered in something black. Timmy started crying. He wanted to get in on the fun.

Andrew crawled back out, put the list onto the desk, got Timmy out of his stroller, sat back down at the desk, and started bouncing him on his knee to make him stop crying. Jealous, Tommy tried to climb climbed onto Andrew's lap as well.

"Damn it, Tommy!" He'd gotten the black stuff all over Andrew's white shirt. Tommy started to tear up, and Andrew, immediately remorseful and not wanting *two* crying kids, pulled Tommy's chair as close to him as possible and *did* make room on the desk for his drawing. "There. Better?" Tommy nodded. And wiped at his eyes.

Andrew scanned the list. Mr. Belsen was at extension 522. He pressed 5-2-2 on the phone. Nothing seemed to happen.

"Hello?"

"Hello?"

"Is this Mr. Belsen?"

"No, just a minute, I'll try again."

He pressed the lit button to put the caller on hold. The light went off.

"Hello?"

He'd disconnected the call.

He put Timmy back into the stroller and started opening the desk drawers to look for some sort of operating manual. And maybe some tissue to wipe Tommy's hands. No such luck. He was about to take him to the washroom when the phone rang again.

"Daddy, I wanna go home now." Tommy had had enough of drawing pictures.

"We can't go home yet, but soon okay?" Andrew said. "Draw another picture?"

"I don't want to!" He threw a highlighter onto the floor.

"Tommy, please don't do that, Daddy has to pick it up now!"

Tommy eagerly clambered out of the chair and started crawling under the desk again.

"No, don't, Tommy, it's all dirty! Come on back up onto the chair."

The phone was still ringing. He picked up the receiver and hit the flashing red button.

"Hello?"

"You cut me off."

"Sorry."

"Is Mr. Belsen there or not?"

"I don't know. I'm trying to connect you."

"I don't have all day."

"Hey, I'm doing my best, okay? Our receptionist isn't here today and I'm filling in for her."

"Well, how hard can it be?"

Andrew pressed a button marked 'Hold' and then pressed 5-2-2 again. Still nothing. He pressed the 'Hold' button again, hoping the person was still there. Nothing. He pressed the 'RLS' button. What did that stand for? Release? As in 'release hold'? No, that didn't make sense. If you had several people on hold, how did it know which one you wanted to release?

"Hello?"

"Hello, Mr. Belsen?"

"No, I'm still trying—"

"Oh for fuck's sake!" the caller hung up.

"Same to you!" Andrew shouted in frustration.

Maybe there was a number to press *before* the in-office extensions, like the number 9 you'd press to get an outside line. During the course of the next eight calls, he tried each one. None of them worked.

Then he noticed the 'TR' button. 'Transfer'? Had to be.

Timmy started crying again. Andrew moved the stroller back and forth, back and forth, but it was awkward handling the receiver and buttons with just one hand. Tommy crawled out from under the desk and started pressing the buttons on the phone.

"Tommy!" Andrew shoved him away.

"I want Mommy!" Tommy started to cry as well. Understandably.

By the time Andrew had a minute to get a cup of coffee, the pot was empty again. Halfway through making another pot, the phone rang again. He ran out to answer it. And this time hit 'TR' before he dialed the extension number. Still didn't work. Damn it! What the hell was he doing wrong? Why couldn't he do this?

Five times he tried to deal with the printer. The first four times, the phone rang before he was halfway across the reception space. The fifth time, he'd opened it up—he'd figured out there were three panels that opened: one on the top, one on the front, and one on the back—but couldn't see anything amiss. Anywhere.

Someone came to stand beside him, several loose pages in his hand. He was a little disconcerted to see Andrew at the machine, but then just said, "Could you make ten copies of this when you get it fixed?"

"What?"

"Ten copies. Thanks." He set the pages on the table beside the printer. Slash copier.

At lunch time, he wanted—well, he wanted to go to lunch. He desperately needed a break. He was hungry. And he still hadn't gotten a cup of coffee. Kyle was right. They'd run out of filters.

And he had to do something with the boys. He'd forgotten Timmy's diaper bag. He hadn't thought to bring any toys, any lunch … Of course, he hadn't known he'd have to bring them in to work …

He popped his head into Simon's office to ask if he'd watch the phones for him.

"Sorry, no can do," he gestured to his own kid, about ten, sitting in the corner on the carpeted floor, playing videos games on his tablet. Then turned back to the "Hot and Hard" website he'd opened.

"Hey, Matthew," Andrew stopped at the next open door. "Would you mind covering me at reception for a few minutes? I've got to get my kids some lunch—"

"Not my problem," Matthew said, shaking his head. Why should he pay the price for someone else's choice? It *was* a choice, after all. To have kids.

So Andrew just left. Let the phones ring. Let them annoy everyone on the floor. And if Richard found out, well, what was he supposed to do, skip lunch?

Yes, apparently. Richard told him as much when he returned. Two hours later.

"If Brittany had pulled that stunt, she'd be fired on the spot!" he thundered at him. Andrew didn't care. One morning on the job and already he was beyond caring.

When he'd left for lunch, he'd driven around, looking in vain for a park, for somewhere he could let the boys run around for a bit, but nada. He passed twenty parking lots, but not one park.

He'd also passed a great many designer and boutique stores, but nothing— He finally spotted a convenience store tucked incongruously between a Gap and a Bath and Body Works, both of which looked closed. In fact, many of the stores had looked closed. Profits are going to take a nosedive, he noted idly, then wondered when the women would be coming back. Where had they gone? He hadn't had any time to consider the larger problem, he realized just then, with surprise. Well, he'd been busy with all the little stuff. There was so much little stuff …

He quickly bought some diapers, some wipes, a few sandwiches, a couple juice boxes, and some cheap toys. He forgot to buy some coffee filters.

On the way back, he finally thought to call Diane's parents' place, just in case. No answer.

The two-hour lunch break had tired the boys enough for them to want to nap, and Andrew had thought to bring the car blanket with him when they returned to the office. He made a hidey hole for them under his desk, laying the blanket onto the floor and then the seat cushion from Sharon's chair. He hoped it would suffice. Fortunately, it did. The boys were asleep in minutes. Amazingly, given the constant ringing of the phones.

By mid-afternoon, Andrew figured out how to transfer a call. By accident. He had to press 'TR' not only before he entered the extension numbers, but also after he'd done so. He'd happened to do that only because he was so harried, he'd forgotten whether he was coming or going.

So he was rather pleased with himself when the flashing red light of the call he'd put on hold in order to transfer it to Mr. Lavigne, at 4-3-3, stopped flashing and went solid. Line 3 rang immediately. He picked up the receiver.

"Hello?"

"I'm on a call!" Mr. Lavigne's voice.

"Oh, excuse me—" Andrew quickly pressed the button for line 3.

"Hello?"

"Could you tell Jack Riley—"

"Hang on, I can transfer you—"

"No, I don't want to talk with him. Just give him this message, darlin', can you do that?"

Andrew stared at the receiver.

"You tell Jack that we're good to go on the nineteenth at six, I've got reservations at the Spear at seven, and he'd better come prepared, you got that?"

Andrew searched for a notepad and pen. "The nineteenth at— what was that?"

At some point, it occurred to him that if after a transfer the light kept blinking, that meant no one was there. He assumed he was supposed to go back on the call and take a message. Right. Like he was going to do that. Like he could figure out how to do that. He tried once, but apparently disconnected the call. Just as well. One of the other lines rang.

When he got home at six-thirty, he was exhausted. More exhausted than he'd ever been at the end of the day. Timmy and Tommy were crying. Timmy needed a change, Tommy's hands were still black, they were both hungry, they were both cranky— But all Andrew wanted to do was to take a long shower, then sit in front of the TV with a bottle of beer, was that too much to ask? Yes. It was, if you had a two-year-old and a four-year-old.

So he changed Timmy, he cleaned Tommy's hands, then made dinner. Of a sort.

"Can we play dinosaurs now?" Tommy asked. "You promised."

"Can't you just play quietly for a while," Andrew begged, "Daddy's tired."

"No, I want to play dinosaurs! DINOSAURS! DINOSAURS!" he screamed.

Andrew would have belted him one right then and there, but he was just ... too damned tired.

It was eight-thirty by the time they were tucked in bed. One of them cried himself to sleep.

Andrew still had to make arrangements for his kids. He'd intended, at some point during the day, to search online for other daycares or a nanny or something, but he hadn't managed to get to it. How could the whole day go by without—he hadn't even checked his email. Not once. Usually, truth be told, he even had time to check the news sites. And do a crossword.

As he reached for his laptop, it suddenly dawned on him that it was Friday. He had the whole weekend to make arrangements. Dead tired, he went to bed. It was only nine o'clock.

2

Saturday morning and part of Saturday afternoon was taken up with the kids and chores. It was a mystery, and a surprise, how doing the dishes, cleaning up the kitchen, straightening the living room, cleaning the bathroom, and doing a couple loads of laundry could take five hours.

Actually it wasn't. Not a mystery at any rate. Timmy and Tommy were constantly interrupting him. They were so needy. How did Diane get anything done? He'd already yelled at them twice. Then immediately regretted it. It wasn't their fault. They missed their mom. They were just little kids. He got that.

The washer stopped working during the second load. When he'd lifted the lid at the end of the cycle to put the clothes into the dryer, he found them sitting in ten inches of water. He called the appliance repair place. Busy.

Then when he returned to the kitchen to properly clean up the juice spill from the previous day, he found Timmy and Tommy merrily putting the ants attracted by the sticky mess into their mouths. He screamed at them. Really screamed. Then locked himself in the washroom for a time-out.

When he called the appliance repair place an hour later, the line was still busy. No doubt someone had simply taken the phone off the hook.

Should he try to fix the washer himself? He stared at it. It was even more impenetrable than the printer had been. Groaning, he pulled it away from the wall and saw a panel at the bottom. Right. Take that off and he was likely to electrocute himself.

He'd try calling again in a couple hours.

Now, now he had to find someone to look after his kids. His first thought was that maybe there was someone in the building. But he didn't know any of his neighbours. His social world was at work.

Was there an apartment directory? He could just start calling. He looked around the apartment and found nothing.

Okay, so he could go door-to-door … No, he'd have to take the kids with him. He sighed. At the moment, doing that … it would be just … too much work.

He decided to go online first. Maybe there was someone in this neighbourhood advertising babysitting services on Kijiji. He was delighted to discover several people doing just that. Katy, Debbie, Irene, Meghan, Melody …

Door-to-door it was. Tommy cowered away from him. It took fifteen minutes of cajoling and then, yes, more screaming, before he got him into presentable shape. No one would agree to look after a tear-streaked, dirty-faced, half-dressed kid. Timmy, thank god, had fallen asleep, so he just carefully transferred him from the couch into the stroller.

Andrew knocked on the first door. No answer. He knocked on the second door. No answer.

"I wanna go home," Tommy whined.

No answers at the next three doors either.

"I wanna go home NOW!" Tommy threatened a tantrum. Andrew ignored him. He thought it best. No, truthfully, he didn't have the energy to do anything else.

The sixth door was answered by someone who could barely

make it to the door. Andrew apologized for having bothered him.

A man in his thirties answered the seventh door. He looked employed. It was worth a shot anyway.

"Hi, I'm Andrew, this is Timmy, and this is Tommy, and I'm wondering whether—whether you know anyone who is available to look after my kids during the day—"

"No, sorry," the man said, closing his door.

Andrew sighed.

"I'll look after your kids," a large man lingering two doors down called out. "Got laid off today," he explained, gruffly, as he unlocked his door.

"Oh—great!" Andrew said. "I mean, I'm sorry—You're—"

"Ivan Keller. I'm a plumber. At P and E Plumbing?"

Andrew shook his head.

"Yeah, they told me business is down. Don't understand it. Just because the women are gone doesn't mean people don't need their toilets unplugged, am I right?"

"You are." Andrew knew why business was down. He was sure he cost Stride Enterprises several new clients on Friday.

"Okay, so, how much do you— How much would you charge?" Wait a minute. He didn't know anything about this guy.

"Eighty-five."

"Eighty-five a day?" Andrew thought quickly. He'd hoped for something closer to fifty a day. But he could probably swing eighty-five. Until— *Were* the women going to come back?

"No," the guy laughed. "Eighty-five *an hour.*"

"An hour? But—"

"That's how much I charge as a plumber. If your kids aren't as important as your toilets and your sinks ..." He stepped into his apartment.

"No, no, they are—" They're *more* important. But eighty-five an hour? Andrew did the math. That worked out to $170,000 a year!

He didn't *make* that much. And even if he did, he needed *something* left over to pay for—everything else.

"You in?" the man was waiting.

"No, I'm sorry, I can't pay that ..."

The man shrugged and went inside, and Andrew wandered distractedly back to his apartment.

He put Timmy in his crib. Tommy agreed to a nap.

The man was absolutely right though, Andrew thought as he sunk into the couch. Surely his kids, anyone's kids, were more important than their toilets. So how was it that plumbers—and electricians, and auto mechanics, and probably tons of other guys— how was it they managed to charge so much? So much more? Because he and Diane sure weren't paying $170,000 for daycare. True, the daycare looked after several kids, but even so, when all was said and done, he doubted that any of the daycare workers made anywhere *near* eighty-five an hour.

He tried calling the appliance place again. Still busy. No surprise. He *knew* it wasn't because everyone's washer had broken at the same time.

He started bailing the washer with one of the kids' toy pails. Then he wrung out each item as best he could before tossing it into the dryer. Took forever.

And by the time forever had passed, it was time to make dinner.

Tommy didn't want peanut butter and jam again. Nor did Andrew. He'd call out for pizza. Surely he deserved it. The line was busy.

"SHIT SHIT SHIT!!" he exploded as he threw the phone across the room. Nearly hitting Tommy and sending him wailing into his room again.

"Tommy, I wasn't aiming at you, Daddy's sorry ..." He started to go after him, but then decided to just let him be.

He opened the fridge, saw that some vegetables in the crisper were about to go bad, figured he could manage pasta, put the veggies into the pot with the pasta and a can of pasta sauce.

Both Timmy and Tommy managed to get the sauce all over their tshirts. Of course they did.

Once the kids were in bed, Andrew popped open a bottle of beer and turned on the TV. He needed to pick up some more beer. When, though? Ordinarily, he'd just go now. But there was no way he could leave a two-year-old and a four-year-old home alone. Tomorrow maybe, on the way to work. No, tomorrow was Sunday. Monday then.

Idly watching *Criminal,* he realized they wouldn't be able to make any more new episodes. Soon there'd be nothing but reruns. No, that's not true, they could just replace the female characters with male characters. Truth be told, there weren't that many, he noticed, relatively speaking, and they were always just minor characters. Mostly they were the victims of some horrible rape or murder. Or rape *and* murder. Sure, *Grey's Anatomy, Madam Secretary,* and *Ellen* would be gone, but those were chick shows anyway.

He switched to the news. Yeah, that would just go back to the way it was when all the anchors had been men. He watched to see if there was anything about the situation. The anchor made a few mistakes. Had the teleprompter been run by a woman? Then there were some glitches about what was to come next. And then some dead air. Cut to a commercial break.

Oh that's gonna change big time, he noted. Advertising.

The news resumed. The women were gone, no one knew how, no one knew why, no one knew for how long. Daycares and elementary schools were closed.

That's it? That was all they had to say?

Guess so. The next item was something about the war in wherever, then there was the business report, which was always something about the economy and the stock market, then the weather report, and then sports. A full ten minutes like usual.

It shouldn't have surprised him. There would be no more shots of gorgeous celebrities in the Entertainment segment of the news, but all of the other segments would go on like before. And why not? The news had seldom been about what women did.

3

Sunday was …awful. He almost went nuts being cooped up in the apartment with a two-year-old and four-year-old. For the second day in a row. But if he went out, he'd have to take them with him, and the mere thought of orchestrating that overwhelmed him.

Early in the morning—before Andrew was up, actually—Tommy had upended the toybox, then had chosen to play with both his police car and fire truck. They both had sirens. Loud sirens. Andrew groaned and rolled over. Then remembered he'd been the one to insist on buying for the boys that very police car and that very fire truck.

When Andrew insisted that playtime was over, Tommy refused to put his toys back in the toybox.

"Don't you want breakfast?"

"NO!"

"Come on, you have to eat breakfast. Help Daddy put the toys back in the box."

"NO!" That was Timmy. He'd finally gotten his hands on the fire truck.

"Yes, please, come on, no more fire truck, Daddy'll read you a story."

"Where Mommy? Mommy read!"

"Mommy's gone." As soon as he'd said it, he knew it was a mistake. "To Grammy's." Too late. Timmy'd started wailing.

Once he'd exhausted himself, Andrew revisited storytime. It did not go well. Timmy kept turning the pages; he didn't care that Daddy hadn't finished the sentence yet. And halfway through, Tommy got his fire truck out of the toybox again.

Andrew sighed, threw the book onto the coffee table, and turned on the TV. To the Kids' Channel.

Monday he decided to call in sick. He thought he'd call HR first to confirm that he did indeed have five sick days left, but there was no answer. So he just went ahead and called Richard on his direct line. As he was dialing, he had a brilliant idea. He could telecommute! That would solve everything. Well, not everything, but—

"I could easily do my work from home," Andrew told him, once he'd made the suggestion.

"As Project Manager, I'm sure you could," Richard replied, "and I'd have no problem allowing you to do so one day a week, maybe even two, but we need our receptionist here. You understand."

"Yes, but I'm not the receptionist."

"You are now," he chuckled.

Why was that funny, Andrew thought to wonder after he hung up.

He had to get out of the apartment. He had to get beer. He had to get groceries. And he had to take Timmy and Tommy with him.

It took the entire afternoon. Half an hour just to get out the door.

The beer store wasn't bad. He left the boys in the car—thank god it wasn't hot—and things were pretty much normal. Except, of course, for the longer than usual lines at the cashiers.

The grocery store, on the other hand, was hell. He put Timmy into the cart, fastening him securely in the baby seat, then told Tommy to hang on.

"Don't let go!" he told him nervously. Why was the store so busy? And so loud?

He started down the first aisle. He hadn't made a list; he thought he'd just cruise and get whatever he saw that he needed. Easier said than done. Everyone who was cruising just like him spent more time looking at the shelves than at where they were going. There were collisions. There were road blocks. No one said 'Sorry' and then moved their cart out of Andrew's way. Instead, people seemed to *intentionally* block not only him, but the whole aisle, belligerently challenging someone, anyone, to say something. After all, they were entitled. They were men.

And, like Andrew, most of the men didn't know where anything was. Their frustration was palpable; they'd clearly had to go down the same aisle several times, first to get this item, then again to get that item. Andrew had done the grocery shopping before with a list, a list Diane had prepared, and he just now realized that she'd prepared the list so the items on it were in the same order in which he'd come to them if he started in Aisle 1 and simply proceeded through to Aisle 8.

"Daddy, get this."

"No, this cereal is better."

"But I want this one!"

"Well, you're not going to get it!"

Tommy let go of Andrew's hand and started to get the box he wanted. Andrew yanked him back, and tugged him along, past the cereal.

They passed a kid in a cart kicking his father.

They passed another kid in a cart screaming so hard his face was red.

They passed a couple older kids knocking stuff off the shelves. Andrew wheeled carefully around several broken glass jars.

Timmy wanted to get out of the cart and walk. Like Tommy. Not on your life, Andrew thought.

When they turned into Aisle 4, they practically bumped into a father hitting his kid. Really hard. Andrew hadn't separated the kid's shriek from the high level of background noise, so the scene took him by surprise.

He tightened his grip on Tommy, then just said to the man, quietly, "Hey." He was ready for "MIND YOUR OWN GODDAMNED BUSINESS!" He was ready to block Timmy or Tommy or both.

Instead, the man just looked at Andrew for a second, dazed. Then a switch seemed to flip on, or off, and he looked at his kid, aghast.

"Oh god, Davey, I'm sorry, I'm so sorry," he sobbed as he picked up his still screaming son and held him close. "Oh, god, Davey, I'm so sorry ..." The two of them sagged to the floor in a mutual meltdown.

By the time Andrew made it through all of the aisles, his cart was full. He double-checked, thinking through the day: coffee, bread, jam, peanut butter, milk, cereal, juice; bread again, cold cuts, tuna, mayonnaise, peanut butter, jam, fruit; frozen dinners, meat, veggies, rice, pasta, pasta sauce; potato chips, cookies. And—he thought of these things only when he saw them—toilet paper, diapers, wipes, paper towels, laundry detergent, soap, shampoo, toothpaste. He also decided to buy a bunch of ready-made stuff at the hot and cold deli counters.

"Anything else, Tommy?" Andrew asked him. Actually, he might know. He always went with Diane. It was an adventure. In a way that today's trip was not. Apparently. In any case, he didn't want get home and then find out that he forgot something the kids considered essential.

"Yogurt," Tommy said, in a small voice. "Mommy always buys yogurt."

Right. But she was the only one who ate it. Nevertheless, it if helped maintain some sense of normalcy … They went back to the dairy section and got some yogurt. And then to the freezer aisle for ice cream. The yogurt had reminded him.

Andrew had noticed, pretending not to, that the line-ups at the only two check-outs that were open went halfway down the closest aisle. It had been difficult to get anything from those aisles and almost impossible to get through to the next aisle. Some men left a gap, but then some asshole always wheeled in to fill it. Andrew had seen the same thing happen on the road. A thoughtful driver would leave a gap so oncoming cars could continue to turn left, or cars coming out of a parking lot could get through, but then there were drivers who would move up and close the gap. *ME* next! His father was like that. Out on the highway, he'd get positively enraged when someone passed him. As if it mattered how many people were ahead of him. As if driving anywhere, everywhere, was a race. He'd actually timed how long it took to get to the family cottage each weekend. That's what happens, Andrew thought, when you see life as a competition.

"Jeezus," Andrew muttered, once he'd manoeuvred into one of the long check-out lines.

"Can't we go now?" Tommy asked.

"No, we have to pay first," Andrew said. "Soon though."

Soon though, my ass, he thought.

He tried to initiate an "I Spy" game with Tommy. No, he just wanted to go home. After ten minutes, Timmy started to fuss. Don't start crying, Andrew pleaded. Please don't start crying.

Half an hour later, they were at the front of the line. And Andrew saw the problem. My god, but the man was slow. It reminded Andrew of how men crossed the street in front of his car. The women always hurried, as if apologizing for making you stop and wait. The men never did. They sauntered across, taking great delight in making you wait. And that seemed to be what the checkout guy was doing. No way he was going to hurry. Not for anyone. He took his bloody time reaching for each item, scanning it, then setting it on the other side.

And then when there wasn't any more room, he'd pack. Instead of packing as he went.

It was painful to watch. He positioned the packages first here, then there, shifting them, repositioning them. And they say men are the ones with the spatial abilities.

When he started to put the heavy carton of ice cream on top of a bag of loose tomatoes, Andrew spoke up. "Wait, that'll crush the tomatoes."

The guy glowered at him. And took the tomatoes out. Then he started to put the hot deli container of scalloped potatoes beside the ice cream.

"It would be better if you put all the cold stuff in one bag, and all the hot in another," Andrew suggested the obvious.

"You wanna pack it yourself?" the man challenged. It was a far cry from the smiling 'Sorry' Andrew normally would have gotten. The 'And how are you today?' had been completely absent.

"It might be better if I did," Andrew said, and started to do so.

The man walked away then, apparently to have a smoke break.

Unfuckingbelievable, Andrew thought. He had to wait for the guy to return so he could pay for his groceries. No surprise that after just two or three minutes of no forward motion, guys several spots down from him starting banging their carts into those of the guys in front of them. Tommy whined. Timmy started crying.

The manager in the office above looked out his little window and decided he'd better hire a security firm. It had actually been suggested by head office the day before, but he'd scoffed at the idea.

As soon as Andrew paid, he went straight to that manager's office to complain. The guy should be fired. Seriously. But no, the manager had no intention of firing him.

Andrew thought then of Richard's comment about how he would have fired Brittany on the spot if she'd taken a two hour lunch. He was sure that if a woman had done what this guy had just done, she also would have been fired on the spot. It's true, he thought, with amazement. Men *do* get away with a lot more shit than women. Women *are* held to higher standards. Diane had always said so, but he had always denied it. How else could you explain the overwhelming number of men in middle and upper management positions? If what she'd said was right, wouldn't *women* be getting promoted over men? It didn't make sense.

Part way home, he realized he'd have to call in sick tomorrow as well. He hadn't had any time to make other arrangements, and by the time he unpacked and then—god, how was he going to get the groceries up into the apartment? Was he supposed to carry one bag at a time in his left hand, pushing Timmy's stroller with the other, making sure Tommy tagged along? It would take ten trips! Tommy would rebel, and rightly so, after just two trips. Could he leave him in the apartment by himself? No, he'd surely start wailing as soon as he closed and locked the door behind him.

Maybe—ah! The shopping carts he saw in the parking garage every now and then! He'd always wondered why someone would take a shopping cart from a grocery store. Now he knew. Still he wondered—would they have wheeled the thing all the way from the store along the sidewalk? Or had some soccer mom with a minivan made a covert run one midnight in order to relocate a few carts for everyone's use?

On his fifth trip—unfortunately, there weren't any carts in the parking garage that day—did the grocery stores come and retrieve them every now and then?—it suddenly occurred to him that he could just call their babysitter! Duh! They paid her only $10/hour. He wondered now, just now, how much people paid boys to cut their grass. He thought it was about $20/hour. Well, that wasn't fair, was it. Unless our lawns are also more important than our kids.

But if he offered $20/hour—which he admitted he should, at the very least—that would … geez, that would be about half his salary. Could that be right? Yes. It would also be more than a year's university tuition for each of the boys. Well, when you thought about it, what universities provided for that money—a couple classes, access to a library and a gym—was nothing compared to looking after a kid for eight solid hours a day, attending to its physical, emotional, cognitive, and social development. So, he supposed $20/hour was—

No, he mentally slapped his forehead, he couldn't just call their babysitter. Alicia would be gone as well. Okay, maybe he could find another high school student, a boy—if the schools were closed—

Were they?

Three hours later—it took that long to get all the groceries into the apartment, then put them away, then make supper, then get the kids to bed—he went online again. Apparently most of the elementary schools were closed, but the high schools were still open.

4

Though 'open' wasn't quite right, since, at least at Central High School, the entrance was guarded and incoming students were frisked. Metal detectors were on order.

"What the hell …" Mr. Archer had murmured as he made his way through the halls to the staff room on that Friday morning. The party atmosphere was unmistakeable. And, for the moment, puzzling.

Eventually he noticed that he wasn't seeing any girls. Then he noticed that he wasn't seeing any women. Come to think of it, he hadn't seen any girls or women on his way in either …

"I tell you it's not going to work!" Mr. Laskey, one of the science teachers, was pacing and wringing his hands. "Best thing to do is close down altogether."

"We can't close down," replied Mr. Nelson, the principal, in a tone that indicated that he thought Mr. Laskey was being a little hysterical about the situation. "It's our responsibility to educate these boys!"

"But there are only, what, fifteen of us?" he looked around the room to count. Ten. The other five must be— Oh god. Several of the ten hustled out of the room, quickly.

"Come on!" one of them said to Mr. Archer as they rushed by him.

Mr. Laskey was right about the math. Female teachers outnumbered male teachers two to one at the high schools. So at nine o'clock, that Friday, two-thirds of the high school classrooms, and halls, world-wide, were 'unsupervised'.

By nine-thirty, at Central High School, Mr. Nelson was on the public address system with a revised timetable that merged classes into an unspeakable horror.

Mr. Yoshi found himself with over a hundred grade twelve Math students in the auditorium. Next period, he'd have the same number of grade eleven Math students. In the afternoon, he'd take the grade ten and nine Math students. He arranged the students in clusters according to where they were in the text, intending to circulate and teach as he went, rather than attempt any sort of lesson per se, but maintaining discipline had been a challenge with thirty students in the room; doing so with over a hundred was impossible. Yes, there was a roster of teacher's aides available to teachers who needed extra help, but well over ninety percent of teacher's aides were women. And so no longer available.

Somehow reading, writing—indeed learning—had become a girl thing. Perhaps because they were typically better at it. Boys acted like high school was all about hooking up and competing. (Given that attitude, and the classroom atmosphere it must have created, and the demands it must have made on the teachers, it's a wonder the girls ever learned anything. Let alone as much as they might have otherwise. No wonder there had been so many advocates of segregated schools.) Now that hooking up wasn't an option, it was full-out competition.

So what started happening that Friday was really no different than what had been happening for quite some time; it was just exacerbated by the situation.

The constant shouting—*real* men spoke up—made it difficult to hear even the students right next to him. The relentless posturing tore his attention away from the task at hand, to make sure it *remained* posturing, so he was seldom able to finish even the shortest of explanations without interruption. And when it escalated beyond posturing? Orders to report to the principal's office were laughed at. Threats of detention were laughed at. And attempts to stop a fight single-handedly were suicidal.

Mr. Corming had a schedule similar to Mr. Yoshi's, but for English, in reverse order, in the cafeteria. He figured it was do-able: he'd teach for half the period, then have silent reading for the remainder. But the first ten students he'd sent to the library to get a book came back—well, seven of them came back—with news that the library was locked. Plan B had been turning English into Home Ec—they'd all be hungry in a couple hours. And of course the cafeteria staff ...

"Let's take a look and see if we can prepare a killer lunch, shall we?"

"Yeah, let's all turn into cafeteria ladies, shall we?" Lewis mocked. "Where are the hairnets, I want a pink one!"

This, from the student most likely to spend his life saying "Would you like fries with that?" In a prison cafeteria.

Once the food fight was over, no one acted on Mr. Corming's suggestion that they clean up—because that's the janitor's job, right?—except for a few of the boys, who figured out that the task provided safety.

One of these boys was James, a smaller than average grade niner, who had been struggling, every day, to get an education. He had been so excited about starting high school, where the real learning happened. In particular, he had been looking forward to studying poetry—*real* poetry, not the stupid rhyming stuff they'd done in grades seven and eight. In fact, he was going to be a poet. He'd already started writing stuff, which he kept in a spiral notebook that he kept with him at all times. Because if his father ever discovered it, he'd make fun of it so much he wouldn't ever want to write another poem.

Plus, the high school had Music, which he'd looked forward to taking. When they got to choose instruments, he thought he'd choose the flute. It was small enough to fit into his knapsack.

But high school was nothing like he'd imagined. The other boys, almost every single one of them, was like his father. They'd mock and jeer. That he could take. Sort of. That is to say, he was used to it.

But when the verbal taunts didn't have their intended effect, the other boys turned to physical taunts. They'd shove him and push him. What did they want? James kept ignoring them, he kept walking away from them, he kept trying to avoid them in the first place, but—what did they want?? Surely they knew he couldn't fight back. If he even tried, they'd beat him to a pulp.

Did they just want to see him cry? He'd obliged them on a few occasions, much to his embarrassment, but the aggression didn't stop. In fact, it got worse.

Unsatisfied with shoves and pushes, they'd started hitting. At first, not very hard, but again, when that didn't have the desired result—*what did they want??*—they started hitting him harder.

So even before that Friday, James had been spending most of his time being on the alert for the worst ones and staying out of sight. It often made him late for class. And then the teachers, who until now had been his—okay, maybe not his protectors, but surely at least his allies—started thinking less of him. It hurt. He'd explained to Ms. Webster why he was so often late for her English class, and she'd believed him, she'd understood, but she couldn't do anything about it.

None of the teachers could, it seemed. At first, some of them tried to stop the fights, but then a knife was pulled on one of them. Mr. Enright ended up in the hospital.

Shortly after that, the teachers stopped sending the trouble-makers—an inadequate word if there ever was one—to the principal's office, for fear of retaliation.

The day the students got their first term report cards, Tyler had screamed into Ms. Webster's face that she was a FUCKING CUNT! He'd received a failing grade. What had he expected? He hadn't done any of the work. But James would understand if Tyler ended up passing the course. It wasn't fair, it wasn't right, but—

He'd heard that the teachers—mostly the female teachers—had asked the principal why he didn't simply expel any student who was physically violent or even verbally abusive. Apparently, Mr. Nelson had laughed, saying that that would eliminate almost half the student body and besides, they all had a right to an education.

The gym was turned into a huge Study Hall. Right. Study. Mr. Berini was hoarse within an hour. And tired of breaking up the fights that seemed to erupt every ten minutes.

The gym classes were taken outside into the field, where Mr. Delven organized a sort of round robin soccer tournament. And pretended not to see the students who simply left. Good riddance to many. Good luck to a few.

Mr. Ellis filled in for the missing vice-principal, Mr. MacKenzie supervised the halls, and the remaining eight teachers were assigned to classrooms, every one of which was overflowing. With male adolescents.

By noon, AV had signed out every single television monitor and its entire supply of movies. Though many kids were just watching whatever they wanted on their laptops and tablets. Watching? No, playing video games. Rehearsing theft, arson, assault, and homicide.

Mr. Tunney had fifty-five students—correction, fifty-five male adolescents—in his chemistry room. He double-checked that the gas to the Bunsen burners was turned off, that the cabinets containing beakers and assorted equipment were locked, and that the room containing the chemicals he used for the year was locked. When he had a moment, he'd suggest to Mr. Nelson that chemistry no longer be offered at Central High.

"Hey, out of my seat!" A boy he didn't know, but knew of, and was certain wasn't enrolled in *any* chemistry course, yanked a younger kid off a stool. And threw him against the beaker cabinet. Fortunately, the glass door held. Which made the boy angry enough to just smash it.

"Hey!" Mr. Tunney called out. But was, of course, ignored. "I want you to report to the principal's office! NOW!" Completely ignored.

He watched helplessly as the boy selected a large shard of glass. And smiled.

Students started running out of the room.

"For later," the boy simply said. Then sauntered out.

Mr. Tunney called the office immediately. No answer. He cautiously stuck his head out his door and looked to the left and then to the right. No bleeding kid on the floor. He made a note to check all the lockers before he left that day. It would be possible for a grade niner to die overnight in one of them. Especially if he'd been slashed.

Which was quite likely because at any given moment, not just every ten minutes, there was at least one fight happening somewhere in the school. It was appalling, really. And would have been an embarrassment had it not been shrugged off as 'boys will be boys'. Hard to see how that attitude persisted when the weapons started escalating, in both number and lethality.

In the bedlam of that first morning, twenty-six kids were seriously injured. And, of course, there was no one in the nurse's office.

By the end of the day, Mr. Nelson called the police station and asked if he could hire a few police officers to be teacher's aides. That was really what they needed anyway: not pedagogical expertise, but … uniformed men with guns. The threat of even more violence. Oh god, he'd moaned to himself, where had they gone wrong?

"While I appreciate your concerns," the Chief of Police had said, when Mr. Nelson had finally gotten through, "we simply don't have any officers to spare."

So Mr. Nelson spent Saturday calling private security companies, then, eventually, just going around in person to the addresses listed in the phone book. He waited in a relatively short line at one such company and was able to hire four men: he put two at the main entrance, locking the other doors, and told the other two to circulate, one per floor, and assist as needed. It wasn't enough.

By the end of the week, he would give up the charade. The high schools had become, and perhaps always had been, just a holding tank for male adolescents.

On Tuesday, James made two mistakes.

"Who knows what density is?" Mr. Archer had asked. Shouted, actually, to be heard over the ongoing rumble in the class. There were fifty students crammed into the room, and since there were only thirty-five chairs, latecomers had to stand. No, that wasn't quite true. Even if you got there early enough to get a chair, someone coming in later could simply take it away from you. James was, of course, one of those standing at the side of the room.

As soon as Mr. Archer asked the question, he raised his hand. Because he knew the answer.

His second mistake was forgetting to peek around the corner later before he turned from one hallway into the next on the way to his second class. He'd been thinking about what density was when it didn't refer to individual things, like people per square yard. When it referred to something like, say, iron, was density a matter of how much there was by weight or how much there was by volume? It had to be by volume, because that's what 'by square yard' essentially meant, right?

As soon as he saw them, he turned and ran, but they were faster. At least, one of them was faster, and that one just hung onto him until the others arrived.

He curled into a ball with his arms wrapped around his head and waited for them to be done. But what hurt the most was that they upended his knapsack, found the spiral notebook, and burned it. Right there in front of him.

Andrew found James huddled on the floor at the end of the hallway

Tuesday afternoon. He'd opened the door to let Tommy run up and down the hall a couple times. It was so much easier than making a trip to the park. Which he'd already done. Twice.

"Hey, are you okay?" He crouched beside him.

James looked up, tears in his eyes. He had a bloody lip and a black eye, and the way he was holding himself suggested he might also have a broken rib or two. His clothing was torn, and his knapsack—Andrew remembered seeing the kid always with a knapsack full of books—his knapsack was gone. Along with, presumably, the key to his apartment. Hence, the huddling on the floor at the end of the hallway.

"Do you want to come wait in my apartment?" Andrew asked. He'd left Timmy there. And had told Tommy to go back inside as soon as he saw—

Just then, James' father came through the door from the stairwell.

"Oh jeezus, what the hell happened to you?" He stared at the boy, clearly disgusted. "You let them beat you up again?"

Again? Andrew was shocked.

"Didn't I teach you how to fight back? D'ya want me to take a few swings at you again?"

Then appalled.

"No," James said in a small voice. "Because I'm not going back."

"Like hell you're not! I won't have you sittin' around here all day like a little princess when I'm out workin' my butt off—"

"I'll hire him," Andrew spoke quickly. James looked at him with hope. With desperation. With 'thank you' screaming from his eyes.

"Yeah? To do what? What the fuck do you think he's any good at?"

"I need someone to look after my kids," Andrew knew it would invite more ridicule, but— "I can't take them to work with me, and—"

The man broke into laughter. "Oh, that's perfect. That's a perfect job for a little sissy boy."

James got to his feet as quickly as he could, wincing.

"When would you like me to start, Mr.—"

"Fraser. And you're …"

"James. Abbot."

"Hi, James," Andrew reached out to shake James' hand. "Would you like to start now? You can come over and meet them, I've got—"

"Sure!" James said all too eagerly. "That's okay?" He turned to his dad.

"Yeah, go, what the hell do I care," the man opened the door to his apartment and went inside.

So James followed Andrew back to his apartment to meet the boys. When he found out how much Andrew was going to pay him, he said he'd do the cooking and cleaning as well. He said he'd do anything, everything, whatever Andrew needed him to do.

"Okay, that's great," Andrew said, trying not to show how overjoyed he was. The boy was in pain. "But first, I think we should get those ribs checked out. I'll drive you to Emerg, okay? An x-ray should tell us whether there's anything broken …"

5

B ut the doors were locked. Chained, actually. Emerg was closed.

On Friday morning, Dr. Harrison had come on shift to find … chaos. The waiting room was overflowing. There was no one at Reception. There was no one in any of the examination rooms. Everyone was clamouring for attention. What the hell?

"Excuse me," a man got up from one of the chairs, "can I get my leg looked at?" He rolled up his pant cuff to reveal a badly infected cut.

"Hey, buster, we were here first," another man holding a child got up and pushed past the first man. "Where do you want us?" he asked Dr. Harrison.

"I think the gentleman over here should be looked at real soon," someone called out. The gentleman in question, seated beside him, was red-faced and sweating profusely.

"Just a minute, everyone, please," Dr. Harrison spread his hands in what he hoped was a 'calm down' manner. "I need— Just give me a minute—" He quickly left the room.

"Hey, where are you going? We need some help here!" the second man cried out.

Where the hell was everyone? Fearing that some fast-acting contagion had knocked everyone out—but why wasn't he finding any bodies?—he raced through Emerg to the East Wing and bumped into Dr. Morris racing from the East Wing to—

"Morris—"

"Will, thank god you're here!"

"What the hell is going on? Are the nurses on strike?" The idea had just occurred to him.

"No," Dr. Morris replied, "at least I don't think so. Bennett's here. But none of the women are. Anywhere."

"What?"

"The women are gone. Didn't you notice the waiting room?"

Now that Morris mentioned it, the waiting room had been full of men. Only men. That never happened. It was usually the mothers who brought in the kids.

"It started happening, oh," he looked at his watch and ran his fingers through his hair, "part way through my shift. Suddenly, there was just Bennett and me. We had our hands full, I've just now done a run through—the East Wing, anyway, and—"

"Are you saying there are *no* women? No nurses? Anywhere? What about X-ray?"

Dr. Morris shook his head.

"The lab?"

He shook his head again.

"How are we supposed to— What are we supposed to—"

"I've been trying to reach the Director, to have him shut down Emerg, but ..."

"What about NICU?"

"I sent Bennett to check it out, then come back."

"Good ... Can he stay? Do a double? Can you?"

"Yes, I think so. Me, yes, certainly."

"Okay, maybe—maybe—did you call all the on-calls?"

"I haven't had time to get a cup of coffee, let alone call all the on-calls!" Dr. Morris protested. He was as frustrated as Dr. Harrison. More, since he'd been trying to deal with the situation for twelve hours now. It's a wonder he was functioning at all.

"Right. Sorry. Okay. Why don't you get a cup of coffee—get me one too—then call all the on-calls— No, wait, surely the Director has done that— Why don't you just come back to Emerg and together we'll clear the room."

"Don't you think— I think I'd better make sure someone's in ICU—and—oh, god, what if someone was in the middle of a surgery—" he took off at a run, leaving Dr. Harrison to manage Emerg on his own. Unless Bennett showed up.

Dr. Harrison returned to Emerg. And didn't know where to start. He had no triage nurse. He had no primary nurse. No physician assistants. No nurse practitioners. He had no charge nurse. Where the hell was the charge nurse?!

He glanced around and chose someone who looked pretty bad off.

"You!" he barked. "This way—" The person got up then promptly passed out. "Nurse!" Dr. Harrison shouted. Out of habit. But no one came running. He wheeled the gurney from behind the door into the room, awkwardly, taking precious seconds, but then he couldn't get the fellow up and onto it. Two others tried to help, but without a backboard, it was hopeless. Dr. Harrison checked his pulse, then just left him there.

"You!" he shouted to the red-faced, sweating man. "This way!"

"Where's your admission form?" Dr. Harrison asked once he'd gotten the man onto the examining table.

"What?"

He hadn't filled out a form. Of course not. He hadn't been given a form. So Dr. Harrison had no history. How could he do his job without a history? How could he make a reasonable diagnosis without— He needed to know about drug allergies, he needed to know the man's blood pressure, he needed to know—

"Name!" he barked.

"Angelo. DiMassa."

Dr. Harrison ran out to Admissions, intending to call up DiMassa's file. He looked at the icons on the screen, searching for one that said Records or some such. Nada. All right, he was a physician. He was nothing if not systematic. He clicked open the first icon. No. He clicked open the second icon. The phone rang. He answered it. Dealt with it. Clicked open the third icon.

A child started crying. Shrieking actually.

He clicked on the fourth icon.

The phone rang again.

"Could you just take a look at this?" someone else had come up to the window. "I may not need stitches after all."

"If you'll just take a seat, I'll be with you in a minute," he said, clicking on the fifth icon, and starting to think he might not need records after all. He could just ask people whether they were on medication, what medication they were on … He could do that while he took their blood pressure. And he could do that while they just died of their injuries.

"Yeah, I've been here since, like, last night."

Dr. Harrison looked up sharply. Six hours was the time frame for stitches. After that—

"How long is this going to take?" someone else had come up to the window.

"I'll be with you as soon as I can!" Dr. Harrison said. Failing to keep the irritation out of his voice.

The phone rang again.

Someone screamed. He looked up in time to see projectile vomit spray the waiting room.

"Housekeeping!" he hollered. No one came running.

That afternoon a middle-aged man rushed into Emerg, saw Dr. Harrison, and simply asked, "What can I do to help?"

Dr. Harrison sighed with relief. "Are you a nurse?"

"No, but surely I can do something." Marcus had been sitting at home trying to think this whole thing through—he was a professor of sociology and gender studies—when it suddenly dawned on him that the hospitals would be hit the hardest *and* would have to be their first priority. "Just tell me what to do."

"Okay, go scrub," he nodded to a sink. "No, wait," he changed his mind, "there's no time for that, just put on a pair of gloves," he nodded to the glove dispenser.

Marcus did as he'd been instructed, then stood beside Dr. Harrison, ready.

"Now as I cut here, you start sponging up the blood—"

At the first cut, Marcus fainted.

"Oh for Christ's sake!"

Bedpans weren't being provided in time. Soiled sheets weren't being changed. Medication wasn't being given on time. Medication wasn't being given, period. IV units weren't being replaced. Oxygen supplies weren't being replaced.

A lone custodian was trying to do what he could up on the fourth floor of the South Wing.

By late morning, every bed in Peds and almost every incubator in the NICU had a stressed-out father sitting beside it, crying, praying, searching online for information.

Elliot, one of the fathers sitting beside one of those incubators, suddenly bellowed. ""HELP! NURSE!" No one came running. "SOMEONE GET A DOCTOR! HE'S TURNING BLUE!"

"That means he's not breathing. Squeeze the bag!" another father called out from across the room.

Elliot squeezed the bag. Too hard, too fast. He blew up his baby's lungs.

By Saturday, all of the on-call and off-duty physicians, surgeons, anestheologists, technicians, nurses, and orderlies had shown up. But it wasn't enough.

On Sunday, the supply rooms were empty. There was surely a central store of supplies somewhere in the hospital, but no one knew where. Needles, four-by-fours, saline solution, local anaesthesia— They needed everything.

By Sunday evening Dr. Harrison had, with varying degrees of gross inadequacy, dealt with four motor vehicle accidents, two workplace accidents, three gunshot wounds, three knife wounds, six assaults, three kids with infections, two cardiac arrests, one broken leg, and two sprained ankles.

And it wasn't until then that he realized that no one had been swooping in to disinfect the examining table between patients.

Elsewhere in the hospital, several people coded. No one had come running.

On Monday, all of the various department heads had shown up, being men, but they had no one to head. No one to carry out their orders. No one to bully. Because, really, did anyone think that any man who had acquired any position of power had done so without such aggressive behaviour? Why else is the norm in business 'Leave your personal ethics at the door'?

It took over an hour for the one ostensibly in charge of supplies to actually think about supplies. And then it took him most of the day to shepherd several carts from each supply room, manoeuvre them into the elevator, wheel them down to Stores, figure out (guess) what was needed, and then return to stock the rooms.

By then, it was mostly too late.

As far as the Director was concerned, women were accessories. That he held that belief, despite incontrovertible evidence to the contrary staring him in the face every day all day, was ... not remarkable. It took him until Tuesday to close the hospital.

The absence of women had brought every hospital to its knees. Within a week. All in all, worldwide, thousands, hundreds of thousands, died. Per day.

And so, finding the hospital closed, Andrew took James to the pharmacy to get something to wrap his ribs with. Even if they *were* broken, he thought, that was probably all the doctor would have done. That and told James to 'Take it easy for a while.' He'd go online when they got back to make sure.

Somewhat to his surprise, the pharmacy was open. Yes, it was a 24/7 pharmacy, but since the cashiers were women, as was one of the pharmacists, he half-expected it to be closed. In fact, the pharmacy *itself* was closed, but the store part was open.

"Hi, can you tell me where I'd find something to wrap broken ribs with?" he asked at the check-out.

"Nope," the young man said, unhelpfully. Without even an apologetic smile.

Why was it, Andrew wondered, as he started wandering up and down the aisles, that women smiled so much more than men? It couldn't be because they were, in general, happier than men. Not if Diane was any indication. And not if their disappearance was in any way voluntary.

He found what he needed, took it to the check-out counter, and paid for it.

"Thanks," Andrew said to the young man. Pointedly. If not sarcastically.

6

I mportant calls only!" the Chief of Police had shouted angrily out the door at the young officer, after he hung up his phone. "I don't have time to deal with high school principals!"

"Yes sir!" The young man at the switchboard was sweating. Literally.

Near as they could tell at the station, the women had started disappearing at around 3:00 a.m. After the bars and the clubs had closed. And when most people were asleep. So unless you were working a night shift, one that involved interaction with women, you wouldn't know until the morning.

As it happened, none of their female officers were on duty that night, so there were no reports of anyone's partner suddenly vanishing into thin air. But when the Deputy Chief on night duty realized that all of his dispatchers were gone, he was certainly puzzled. He immediately contacted the on-call dispatchers. None of them answered their phones. Even more puzzled. Then he thought to contact a few of their on-call female officers. None of them answered their phones either. What were the odds? That's when he contacted the Chief. Got him out of bed at 4:00 a.m.

By 5:00 a.m., the Chief had established that the situation was nation-wide. At least at police precincts.

By 6:00 a.m., he'd made a request to the powers that be to declare a state of emergency. He'd also requested the assistance of the national guard, the army reserves … something. Unfortunately, the powers that be weren't nearly as forward-thinking.

"Stress levels are going to be way up," the Staff Sergeant was saying to the officers about to head out for patrol. "Men are trying to cope, trying to cover for— Expect … everything." He sighed. This was going to be a helluva day. He honestly wondered how many of his officers would survive it.

"And I don't have to tell you that the criminal element will know we're spread a little thin, what with having to reassign several of you to desk duty. They'll consider this an opportunity."

"Yeah about that," one of the men spoke up. "You'll be rotating us, right? I'm not driving a desk for the rest of my life."

"We've contacted the Academy and we'll be advertising, to fill the positions with cadets and civilians, but it'll take time. They have to be trained in protocol. An arrest is useless if the chain of evidence is botched. You all know how important it is that we follow the regs. It doesn't help that we're now down a couple training officers. We've got IT taking a look at our 911 system, to increase the automated responses, but we can't go too far on that. And we can't automate dispatch."

"They should be telling people to just stay indoors!"

"I'm sure they're working on public service announcements, but …" he trailed off. He wasn't sure of any such thing. "We'll have you back on the street as soon as we can."

"In the meantime," someone spoke up, "maybe a couple of us can patrol solo."

The Sergeant wasn't sure that was a good idea, but in the end decided that it was better than having whole areas without any police presence whatsoever.

The solo patrols never came back.

"What the ...?" an officer muttered in disbelief, as he and his partner cruised down a street. Alarms were screaming, windows were broken, fire hydrants were spraying ... "It's like a fuckin' war zone."

Men's propensity to respond to any stress whatsoever with violence—against person, against property—without reasonable rationale—was all too clear.

His partner ventured an explanation. "Mom's gone?"

By noon, they were responding only to life-threatening situations. Not missing persons. Not thefts. Not even simple assaults. Thank god domestic disputes were out of the picture.

But it took until the end of the month to establish martial law. Pretty much worldwide.

7

Although panic ensued elsewhere at the university— Admissions, the Registrar's Office, Student Services, Financial Aid, Alumni Fundraising, Academic Advising, Career Services, Special Needs, Food Services—in Marcus' little corner of academia, nothing much had changed. Half of his students were gone and one-third of his colleagues, but he could continue pretty much as before.

Interesting numbers, he thought. But not surprising. If half of all Sociology graduates, for example, were women, half of all sociologists should be women. But somehow the male graduates always ending up getting the lion's share of the positions. It wasn't right. It wasn't fair. Especially since his female students were typically better. They were the ones who got the As. His male students didn't seem to think they needed to work as hard. And they were right, of course.

Study after study, for decades, had shown that men have higher incomes than women. In fact, it wasn't unusual for male *high school* graduates to be paid more than female *university* graduates. And no, it couldn't be explained, not completely, by 'Women leave the work force to have kids and, thus, lose seniority.' Even if using seniority as a criterion for raises and promotions was justified. Which, until time on the job by part-timers *counted* in seniority calculations, it wasn't.

No, the reason was clearly sexism: we value what men do more than we value what women do. Back in the 70s, researchers gave a young man and a young woman the very same resume, coached them to answer questions with the very same answers, and so on, then sent them out to job interviews. The young man was offered an entry level middle management position, and the young woman was offered a job as a receptionist. Every single time. Variations of the study had been repeated since, most recently at Yale, and the results had remained the same.

Similar studies ask students to evaluate an essay: the one by 'John' is consistently ranked higher than the one by 'Jane' even though the essays are identical.

In yet another study, one group of college students is asked to complete a paragraph which begins 'After one semester, John finds himself at the top of his medical school class …' Another group is asked to complete a paragraph which begins 'After one semester, Anne finds herself at the top of her medical school class … Guess which fictional person ends up having an outstanding academic and professional career. When a social studies teacher repeated the study with her high school class, two boys, working independently, wrote that Anne was run over by a truck.

But oh no, Marcus grimaced, we don't need feminism anymore, we're living in a post-feminist world. Sure we are.

Of the colleagues who were gone, he especially missed Addison, who had been doing wonderful work in genetics, Liz, who was a stats whiz, and Aiko, whose music had always moved him.

And, of course, his teaching partner, Beth. The university had a Gender Studies program, in addition to their Women's Studies program, and he and Beth team-taught the Introduction to Gender course. They thought it best to team teach the course, with one male professor and one female professor, not because they thought gender was hardwired and they wanted one of each at the helm so to speak, but because the male professor would have a lifetime of experience as a man and the female professor a lifetime of experience as a woman. Though even that ... Experiencing a thing didn't mean you had any insight into the thing. Which is why he figured he could call himself a feminist. You don't need to be black to see, to understand, racism and be against it. And just because you *were* black didn't mean you *did* understand it. Though actually, Marcus didn't consider himself so much feminist, as anti-sexist, anti-gender. In a nutshell, his view was that one's sex should matter only in a few select medical contexts. It should, generally speaking, be about as big a deal as eye colour.

However, perhaps the most significant reason for the decision to team-teach the course was that they wanted to attract male students as well as female, and they thought that having the mixed team would be most likely to do that.

Unfortunately, in their class of 43, only six students were male. And half of those seemed to have enrolled just to challenge, and antagonize, and assert their dominance—not to learn. Those three students would hog the floor, talking on and on as if they were the only students in the class, as if they were entitled to most of the air time. They'd interrupt every woman who tried to speak, talking over them, drowning them out. Their swaggering confidence intimidated, and their derisive tone silenced. In short, they did everything Dale Spender said men did.

So he and Beth assigned Spender. The students—those three—denied her claims. So four of the students—two of the other men and two of the women—did a study of their own class. And found the same results. The men talked more than the women. The men interrupted more than the women. The men 'mansplained'. And still, the three men still denied it.

It was a real problem. At first, he and Beth engaged with what they said, but when they pointed out their lack of evidence, their dependence on anecdote, their red herring mistakes, their paper tiger mistakes, their overgeneralizations—well, it was just so bloody exhausting.

"Today," Beth would start, "we'd like to talk about Babcock and Laschever's hypothesis that one of the reasons women are paid less than men is that they don't ask for more. They don't negotiate their opening salary, and since subsequent raises are based on—"

"They don't get paid as much because they're not worth as much," Asshole #1 interrupted.

"No, that's exactly the view that their research seeks to disprove, because—"

"Their work isn't as difficult!" Asshole #2 jumped onto the bandwagon.

"Or as important!" Asshole #3.

"Okay, so you've—among the three of you—you've proposed two or three alternate explanations for the wage gap, and we can discuss those in a minute, but first, I'd like to stick with the reading—did you do the reading?"

Silly question. Of course not.

"May I suggest that until you do the assigned reading, you refrain from participating in the discussion—*of* the assigned reading?" It was a perfectly reasonable request.

"Are you saying I don't have a right to participate in class? I paid my tuition, same as everyone else!" Asshole #2.

The rest of the class groaned.

Beth ignored the comment. "As I've said, Babcock and Laschever propose that women simply don't ask for more. When they're given a salary figure, they just accept—"

"It's their own fault they don't ask for more, isn't it?"

"Okay, let's look at that. What reasons do the authors give for not asking for more?" She looked out at the class, inviting participation by the others.

"For starters," one woman ventured, "it's because—"

"All's I know," Asshole #1 interrupted, seemingly oblivious to the fact that someone else had spoken, and in a tone suggesting that, really, this was all he needed to know, "is that they already get more than they deserve, why should we give them more?"

"Okay, on what basis are you claiming that they don't deserve more?" Marcus would ask, trying to—

"On the basis that if they did, they'd already *get* more."

"All right, that's an example of a circular argument. Do you remember what a circular argument is? Anyone?"

No one would say. Even though everyone knew. Except Assholes #1 through #3.

"A circular argument is one in which you use your conclusion as a premise. You assume at the beginning the very thing you're trying to prove by the end. Trevor, what are you trying to prove? What's your conclusion?"

Silence.

"Okay, I can help you out here, your conclusion is that—"

"I don't need your fucking help—"

"Well it seems that you do, because—"

"I know lots of women, too fucking many—"

"We've asked you before, Trevor, to please refrain from profanities in the class."

"'Please refrain from profanities'," he mocked Beth's tone. "I know lots of *fucking* women who speak up for what they want."

"That may be, but we're talking generalities here," Marcus would say. "Remember the value of anecdotal evidence. Babcock and Laschever's hypothesis is that *in general*, women are conditioned to be quiet, to be non-assertive, to wait until they're asked, whereas men are conditioned to speak up, aggressively, whenever they want, for whatever they want, and as a result—"

"That's a load of crap."

"And yet," Beth would point out, "this very class seems to support their claim."

Not only was it exhausting, it was time-consuming: by the time they'd finish fully addressing each comment the three of them had made, there was never enough time to cover the material they'd intended to cover. They couldn't afford to keep being derailed.

The three of them didn't care anyway. They didn't really listen to his or Beth's dutiful, thorough responses; they'd just interrupt with another off-argument comment.

He and Beth had had numerous conversations about what to do. Eventually they decided to let the three of them talk uninterrupted until they were done and then just completely ignore what they'd said. That seemed to work: most of the time, they didn't even realize their comments had been ignored; that's how insincere they were about them. But Marcus was worried that one day one of them *would* realize he wasn't getting the attention he felt oh-so-entitled to—and would demand it. With a semi-automatic.

He saw the same sort of thing on feminist blogs. Men would show up and post such incredibly ill-considered comments, it would take the others an enormous amount of time and effort to respond to them—to explain why the comment was irrelevant or why it wasn't the refutation they seemed to think it was or what basic bit of knowledge or understanding was missing ... Eventually most blog communities developed a shortcut response like 'This isn't Feminism 101' or 'I'm not responsible for your education' or 'Come back after you've done your research'—but such responses served only to enrage the commenter who would then scream 'Feminazi!' Or worse.

They called it trolling, but he thought that gave the posters too much credit. Most such men weren't *intentionally* derailing the conversation. They really, simply, *were* that clueless—to the rules of reasoning, to the principles of relevance, and, in this case, to sexism and the patriarchal system that made such cluelessness possible, virtually mandatory.

Given the 'or worse', Marcus often wondered what would have happened if he *hadn't* been part of the teaching team, if Beth had had to deal with those three students on her own. He had no doubt that at the very least, the three of them would have gone to the Dean to complain about her: perhaps they'd say she was biased, pushing her feminist agenda; perhaps they'd say she didn't respect their opinions, their completely unsupported opinions; or perhaps one of the other students would finally have enough and complain that she wasn't a good teacher, she couldn't control the class. He'd seen it happen again and again. Well, no, he'd never actually *seen* it, since he was a male professor, and the sort of thing that happened in the IntroGen class *never* happened in any of his Sociology classes, but he'd heard that it had happened again and again. And the woman in question would be, essentially, fired; technically, not rehired, since she'd most likely be a sessional. If she was an assistant or associate, she probably wouldn't get tenure.

Quite apart from *that* sort of career block, no wonder women achieved less than men: to have to deal with all of that *and* keep up your research program, write your papers, seek publication?

Though, Marcus realized, even *without* having to deal with all of that, the woman probably wouldn't get tenure. Men stacked the deck in their favour in terms of what counted and what didn't.

That Friday, he stumbled through the day, like most people, perplexed and, as the day went on, increasingly alarmed. About the women, about the men. About what had happened, and about what was going to happen.

He spent the weekend at the hospital. After demonstrating his unsuitability as a surgical nurse, he simply went from room to room, doing whatever he felt competent to do. Which, admittedly, wasn't much …

"Unbelievable," Marcus murmured that Sunday evening as he watched yet another newscast in which the situation was barely mentioned. It was unnerving, the lack of coverage. The world should be hearing from fine minds of all stripes.

All right, he told himself, step up!

Okay, but at the moment, he had nothing but conjecture.

So get more.

8

Monday, Marcus went door-to-door trying to line up an interdisciplinary team of scholars interested in investigating the situation, specifically, the short- and long-term effects of the absence of women. He wasn't qualified to investigate how they had disappeared, where they had gone, or when, or even whether, they'd be back, nor could he do anything more than hypothesize about why they had disappeared—but he could certainly study the effects of their absence.

He had read the article in *Macleans*, showing that virtually half of the men surveyed said they didn't consider themselves feminist. And that was *after* they were given the definition of 'feminist' as simply "someone who believes in the social, political, and economic equality of the sexes". He couldn't believe it. For him, the question was a no-brainer.

So most men, and many women, thought women were inferior? How could that be? Why would they think that? The researchers hadn't asked why. Did people think women weren't *capable* of *handling* equal social, economic, and political power? Because, perhaps, they weren't *educated* to *be* capable of social, economic, and political equality? But, he said to himself, let's be honest: neither are men. Did they think they didn't *deserve* equality? What had women done to make them think that? Why did so many women themselves think that? He had been, in a word, flabbergasted.

Furthermore, the magazine had said that the roughly 50% that *did* consider themselves feminist was "more than one might think." *More?* So *Macleans* had expected *less* than half of the population to believe in women's social, economic, or political equality? Was he so out of touch?

Apparently. Because he had thought that the not-feminists would be the less educated. Surely among intellects such as himself …

He should have known better than to start with Philosophy.

"Hi there," he said, poking his head into the first office with an open door. A grey-haired man swivelled his chair away from his computer to face Marcus. "I don't think we've formally met," Marcus continued, entering the office with his hand extended, "I'm Marcus Epherine, over in Sociology."

The man reached across his desk and shook his hand. But said nothing.

"I'm wondering whether you might be at all interested in joining a research team to investigate the short- and long-term effects of the current situation."

The man looked at him. "And what situation might that be?"

Marcus stared at him. When all of the women in world had disappeared, what other 'situation' might he be referring to?

"The women's disappearance."

The man smiled, waved his hand vaguely, as if Marcus were pulling his leg, and turned back to his computer screen.

Marcus was puzzled. To put it mildly.

He went on to the next office and received a somewhat similar response. Amusement and disinterest, with a faint whiff of offense.

The third and fourth offices were empty.

At the fifth office, he opened with, "Philosophers *do* research, don't they?"

"Yes," the youngish man smiled, half-got up out of his chair and extended his hand. "Hi, I'm Jeremy Villings, Theories of Justice."

"Hi," Marcus shook his hand, "Marcus Epherine, Sociology. And Gender Studies."

"Please to meet you. What brings you to our neck of the woods, asking whether we do research?" Jeremy grinned, nodding at the empty chair beside his desk.

"Well," Marcus took a seat, "I'm trying to line up an interdisciplinary team to investigate the effects of the women's disappearance, and I thought it would be good to have a philosopher on board, but the two I've approached so far seem ... not to have taken me seriously, I suppose you might say."

"Yeah, I'm not surprised," Jeremy said, "but it's not you."

"Oh, that's a relief, perhaps, but then—"

"It's kind of the kiss of death in Philosophy to have anything to do with women—Philosophy of Women, Philosophy of Gender. Real philosophers go into Logic, Epistemology, that kind of thing."

Real philosophers?

"What about Ethics?" Marcus asked.

"Ethical *theory* is okay, but *applied* ethics ... again you're getting into the soft there ..."

The *soft*?

"And theories of justice?"

"Yeah," Jeremy conceded, "it was a bit of a risk, but Rawls is a heavyweight, and he takes a principled approach, rational choice and all that, with a sprinkling of economics—"

"And those are *hard* things? Male things? Good things?" Marcus was trying to put it all together.

"I guess you could say that," Jeremy was only slightly embarrassed to hear it put so baldly.

"I see," Marcus said as he left, calling back a "Thank you" but not bothering to ask Jeremy about his interest.

Just before Beth had left—disappeared, he corrected himself—she'd mentioned a website titled *What Is It Like to be a Woman in Philosophy?* He found it that night.

> "I was excited and nervous to discuss my project-in-progress. One of the first bits of feedback he gave me was that I would make a good mother."

> "Today I was in my office catching up on some grading. My door was open and a faculty member at another campus location whom I have never met came by to talk about an undergraduate symposium I was organizing. He stuck his head in, saw me at my computer, surrounded by papers, and said 'I don't suppose Professor X (me) is in, is he?'"

> "My department at the time was hiring, and they whittled down the shortlist to four candidates. Each candidate was to present a paper to the general public (in reality only the department members and interested students would attend). They then would make the final decision of hiring with that presentation in mind. I only attended this particular female philosopher's presentation because I was interested in the topic, and did not attend anyone else's.

> "I do not remember much about the content of the paper, but I remember *vividly* the reception of the paper. It was absolutely hostile. Right off the bat the first question was very critical, and there was no relent. There was no

woman department member present, as far as I can remember."

"I am a middle-aged woman who regularly teaches a course in the history of modern philosophy. I use standard anthologies on the topic and present a survey from Descartes to Kant. More than once I have been 'corrected' by undergraduates on my choice of materials for the course."

"I arrive on time for my presentation, set up everything, and notice that the audience is almost entirely made of mature male academics. Before I start my presentation one of them loudly refers to me as 'young lady' and after I start my presentation he interrupts me and asks me to speak up because my 'voice is too weak'. The questions session is dominated by condescending and dismissive questions. No woman asks a question. After a while people start leaving the room. Eventually the chair says they are very busy with work the next day and leaves. Despite my attempts, I am never reimbursed for the trip."

After a mere half hour of reading through the most recent posts, Marcus had enough.

Then he imagined what it would be like to not just *read* about it, but to *experience* it. And not just for half an hour, but for your entire life.

To say he was surprised would be an understatement. He'd thought that of all disciplines, the one that housed logic, the one that had popularized critical thinking, the one whose graduates scored the highest on the GRE and the LSAT, would be the *least* misogynistic, the most able to see the illogic of it all. On the contrary, it seemed that of all the humanities, Philosophy was the *most* misogynistic.

Yes, he was vaguely aware of the misogyny of Aristotle, Rousseau, Kant, Hegel, Nietzsche—but this was the 21st century!

Curious, he took a look at some of the upcoming conferences, one of which was titled "And Justice for All". Not one of the scheduled presenters was a woman. Probably an all-white list too, he thought. Another conference, "Philosophizing the Future", again, featured not one woman. Did they not even *see* the irony?

Marcus discovered that Economics, though not in the humanities, was a close second.

"You aim to get behind Marilyn Waring and her ilk?" Professor Charles Serrento asked, after Marcus had delivered his opener. "Oh I wouldn't advise that, no."

What? Marcus was, again, puzzled. How does wanting to study the effects of the women's disappearance imply that one endorses Marilyn Waring? Ah. The man would have to be thinking that women are some monolithic mass, unindividualized. Jeezus.

Marcus had heard of Waring, of course, but he hadn't actually read her stuff. Curious, he went to the library, signed out *If Women Counted* and read it that night. Her work had persuaded the United Nations to redefine the Gross Domestic Product—and *still* Serrento *dismissed* her? Unbelievable.

Marcus added Waring's book to the recommended reading list for IntroGen. The list was already impossibly long, but ... *everything* was about gender, it seemed.

Psychology was considerably better.

"Hey, Marcus, isn't it?"

"Yes, Gaston? Gerard? Sorry ..."

"Gustave. Come in, what can I do for you?"

"I'm trying to put together an interdisciplinary team to investigate the effects of the women's disappearance."

"Ah. Grief on a massive scale. Especially among the older generation. In fact, I wouldn't be surprised to see many men simply passing on. It often happens that when one spouse passes, the other goes soon after."

Marcus nodded. He hadn't even considered this, he was so used to looking at things on a societal scale.

"Then again, when you consider that half of all marriages end in divorce, I think it's safe to say that at any given time, half of the population *wants* to divorce, so I'd predict that half of the married men under, say, sixty, are secretly relieved."

"Really?" Again, Marcus hadn't considered this at all.

"Yes. If not for inertia, I think we'd be seeing a lot more divorces. And of course," Gustave continued, "happily married or not, men would be missing their daughters. The younger, the deeper the felt loss."

Again, Marcus hadn't—he hadn't even *thought* about fathers missing daughters. He himself was single and child-free.

"Now, the *unmarried* men, there's your greatest danger. The frustration, the sense of having been cheated, if you will ..."

Marcus nodded. *That* he had anticipated. Masses of young men wandering the malls ...

"Have you heard of 'the last generation phenomenon'?"

Marcus thought for a second, then shook his head. Serrento had spoken about *lost* generations—if the women didn't come back soon, there would be one or more lost generations which would play havoc with the supply and demand of the labour force, not to mention the national pension fund. Marcus had been incredulous. After everything that had been happening, this man, this *intelligent* man, was still seeing women, *defining* women, by their biology. Even more specifically, even more limiting, by their *reproductive* biology. What does it take, Marcus had wondered.

"There's a hypothesis," Gustave explained, "and there was a novel, or maybe a movie, based on the premise that when a generation discovers itself to be the last generation, everyone just sort of gives up, everything goes to hell in a handbasket. I'm not convinced that so many people find purpose only in future generations, but …"

"Certainly our destruction of the environment challenges that view …"

"It does. Or would, if people really thought the environment had been destroyed."

"You don't think they do?"

"No. Not until they themselves have no food or water. Consider the thinning ozone. That's been going on since the 70s, and yet … Dangers have to be clear and immediate to be believed. By most people."

"So if air pollution were a visible black haze, or if acid rain stung, or if we could actually see holes in the sky …"

Gustave nodded.

"That lack of … imagination? Effort? To just think about it? It's disturbing, isn't it."

"It is."

"So, would you be interested in joining the team? Can I put your name on the proposal?"

"Sure," Gustave said. "Why not?"

Anthropology was outstanding.

Dr. Hainswarth practically shouted, "But of course!"

Marcus was delighted.

"This 'situation' as you put it," Hainswarth went on, nodding to an empty chair for Marcus, "is a dream come true for us anthropologists. We get to study, up close and personal, perhaps the first, perhaps the only, male-only society. Until now, this has been the realm of science fiction!"

Marcus sat.

"Every one of our grad students has already scrapped whatever they were working on," he chuckled. "They're all madly drawing up new research proposals, and I can't wait to see what they come up with.

"And the international community, my goodness, we're all a-buzz! There are joint committees and conferences and projects underway—perhaps I should be asking *you* if you'd like to join one of *our* research projects!"

Marcus considered that. "I'm honoured, but— Is there a feminist anthropology subdiscipline?"

"There is, but its focus is on reducing male bias in the practice of anthropology," Dr. Hainsworth went to his book case and started scanning the titles, "and I'm not sure how that relates to ..." He turned to Marcus. "You said you were Sociology and Gender Studies?"

"Yes."

He turned back to his bookshelf. "Elsie Parsons, she's one of the big names in feminist anthropology ... She began in Sociology, I believe ... but she's first wave ... aha!" He pulled out two books and gave them to Marcus. "You might want to contact Gayle Rubin and Sherry Ortner—oh." He sat down heavily. "For just a minute, I—" He looked up at Marcus, tears in his eyes.

The next day, Marcus thought he'd try his luck in the faculty lunch room, see who was there, see what might come of unplanned conversation ... But as soon as he entered, he remembered why he never ate in the faculty lunch room. All of the men were sitting on one side of the room, and— It was as if they were still in high school, boys on one side, girls on the other side. Now, of course, there was just empty space on the other side. He shook his head in disgust, and sadness, then turned, and left.

By the end of the week, Marcus had completed his application for internal funding and had delivered it in person to the Office of Research Services. Completing the application for external funding would take longer.

It would be weeks, maybe even months, before a decision was made.

In the meantime, he could offer informed conjecture, so he started writing letters to various newspapers. They didn't get published. He started writing articles for various magazines. They didn't get published. Editors called him a feminist sympathizer. As if that was a bad thing.

He started calling radio stations, offering to be interviewed. He did better with radio interviews than with television interviews. Once people saw how short he was, they immediately dismissed him. It was irrational. And, so, it was infuriating. And yet, it just occurred to him that almost all women are, were, shorter than him, shorter than almost all men. Was height another reason for their subordination? What if women were, on average, *taller* than men? The Tutsi-Hutu conflict popped into his head: the Tutsi had greater economic wealth than the Hutu; the Tutsi had greater social status than the Hutu; the Tutsi subordinated the Hutu; and the Tutsi were taller than the Hutu.

So why did even women dismiss him? Because, he reminded himself, experience doesn't necessarily confer insight. He thought of all the women he knew who *weren't* feminist. Or who *claimed* to be feminist because they wanted sex and said so and dressed so and had it with whoever they wanted whenever they wanted—as if sexual agency was all there was to feminism, had anything to do with feminism. And as if men didn't just take them for sluts anyway. As far as he was concerned, and Beth had vehemently agreed, 'SlutWalk' was the disaster of the century, perhaps the worst thing ever to have happened to the feminist movement. (What they'd needed, Beth had maintained, was a 'Fuck Femininity!' walk wherein women took to the streets just looking like they looked and wearing whatever was comfortable.)

And the princesses in his classes. Oh god, they were as bad as the assholes.

But then why shouldn't women make the same mistake as men, screaming they had rights (especially since feminism told them they did!) (never mind that they didn't know they used to *not* have those rights—the right to vote, the right to own property, the right to attend university, the right to obtain contraception ...) and forgetting the strings attached, forgetting the responsibilities that were attached to those rights.

9

B y mid-week, Darryl had had enough. Even before he hit the road to head home.

He was okay with Elise working in the department, equal opportunity and all that, but now that she was gone, he was put back on routine installs and upgrades. Not troubleshooting. It was boring. It was beneath him. Two bloody weeks now he'd been doing nothing but installs and upgrades.

And then to make matters worse, his supervisor had reamed him out because he wasn't doing as many as she had done in a day. Apparently Little Miss High Achiever had been doing a whopping 50% more than him. Dickhead Dick had shoved his little Productivity Analysis in his face. He could shove it up his ass for all he cared.

"When she comes back, you're going to keep *her* job, and she's going to get *yours*," he shouted, then muttered something about correcting the post-war mistake. "In fact, I should have given her your job long ago, you've been a slacker from the beginning."

"It's taking me so long," Darryl protested, "because the schedule's all messed up!" He kept going to the wrong office. Yeah, okay, sometimes he just read the numbers wrong, but what was he supposed to do, wander around the whole fucking building, knocking on everyone's door asking if they needed IT? Fuck that. He wasn't a girl scout selling cookies.

So when the car behind him rear-ended him, he lost it. He rear-ended the car in front of him. Then backed up a bit and did it again. And again. And again.

The guy in the car beside him, who happened to be Marcus, looked over with raised eyebrows that clearly said "Seriously?"

Darryl gave him the finger. Actually, he gave him the whole fisted arm.

Jeezus, Marcus thought. Then hoped like hell that the guy being repeatedly rear-ended didn't have an infant in a car seat in the back.

Such road rage, hell, such *rage*, wasn't unusual now. Like Andrew, Marcus had definitely noticed the increase in aggression and violence. The increase in *male* aggression and violence. Best label it correctly. And he'd been thinking about it. He was close to concluding that the old bouncer wisdom was correct: 'They're either going to fuck or fight.' And now that the first was impossible …

Or was it simply that now that men had lost their regular punching bags, they were venting their rage on each other. And more often, he refined. If that were possible. Which apparently it was. Or at least, more publicly, he revised.

Or maybe it was that without their personal cheerleaders, without an audience dedicated to their every move, they had become more insecure, so they had more need to prove themselves.

Speaking of which, most men had no idea how much emotional work women did. Most men didn't even know emotional work was needed. For themselves, personally, and for society as a whole. They *certainly* didn't know how much most women resented *doing* most of the emotional work.

Once Darryl's tantrum had run its course, he reached for his cell phone. In the event of an accident, you were supposed to call the police right away and not move your car, right? The guy behind him had rear-ended him. Accident.

No answer. He let it ring and ring and ring.

The guy in front of him must be doing the same, he thought, half-snickering. The world is fucked up, that's for sure.

Finally the guy who'd rear-ended him got out of his car with a piece of paper. Right. They could exchange insurance company names or whatever. He pulled out one of his business cards and wrote the name of his insurance company on it. Did the same for a second card. Then he got out of his car, intending to give one to each guy. Then he saw the guy in the car ahead of him get out of his car and reach into the back. Darryl quickly changed his mind, got back in, and engaged his door locks.

The guy had a baseball bat.

Andrew, a couple lanes over, and able to keep moving, saw what was happening. He didn't bother reaching for his cell phone. He knew there was a police station just ahead. He's stop and notify them of the situation. In case they weren't already aware of it.

He took the next exit, then the first left to the station. His eyes widened as it came into view. The station seemed to be under assault. Or riot. Or something. What the fuck?

"Hang on!" he shouted to the boys and made a U-turn without slowing down.

It wasn't enough that the cunts fucked up everything when they *were* here, Darryl was still fuming as he pulled into the underground lot at his apartment building. They were fucking it up even when they *weren't* here.

Like that feminazi, what was her name, Parsimian or Sarkeesian or something, that bitch who did all that screaming about online gaming and how all the female characters are nothing but T & A. Big whoop. She should mind her own business. It was all just games, for Christ's sake, who the fuck cares if all the chicks have big boobs? And so what if the characters get roughed up a bit, it doesn't mean anything. Gamers are only trying to have a little fun, since when is that a crime?

At least she got what she had coming to her, he laughed. Someone had constructed a game in which *she* was the bitch who got it good. He hadn't heard about the death threats that had made her cancel several lectures. One guy had promised a repeat of the Montreal incident, vowing to kill as many feminists on campus as he could. Darryl would've cheered.

Perhaps more importantly, he didn't believe the studies that showed that what you watched on TV and online affected your attitudes, your beliefs, which in turn affected what you did in real life. Or wouldn't've believed the studies. He didn't know about them. Doesn't matter. He wouldn't've cared.

Darryl had gotten home late, the road had taken forever to clear, but he had nothing to do on Friday nights now anyway. At every single club, nothing but guys. What was he supposed to do, start batting for the other team?

Thank god most ITers were still men. The internet was still working just fine thank you very much. A lot of sites were down, but all the important ones were good to go, he snickered, settling onto his couch with his laptop. And loosening his pants.

10

Next day, Darryl called his insurance company. He was, of course, shunted into an automated answering system. He dutifully listened to the menu, then hit '1'. Then listened to another menu, then hit '3'. Then listened to a third menu, then hit '2': speak to a claims officer.

But he didn't get to speak to a claims officer, not even after waiting a full five minutes. Eighty percent of them had been women.

So he took a long lunch, Dickhead Dick could suck on it, and went to the company in person. Stood in a long line for a long time. But finally got to the front and was given a claims form on a clipboard to fill out.

He left the counter, wandered to the crowded reception area, standing room only, and filled it out.

When he returned to the counter, the man just took the completed form from him and added it to a pile. A tall pile.

"That's it?" Darryl asked. He'd expected to speak with someone.

"What more do you want?" the guy asked. Sullenly.

"Can you tell me how long it will take to process my claim?"

"Nope." It was almost as if he was *trying* to do a bad job. Because customer service was a woman's job and if he did it well, that would mean he was … a pussy.

"What am I supposed to do in the meantime? Get my car repaired and send you the bill?"

"Sure. You do that." The man laughed.

"What's that supposed to mean?"

"What's what supposed to mean?"

"That laugh."

"It means you can send the bill, but don't expect reimbursement any time soon," he gestured at the near-empty office.

"It means," the guy behind Darryl said, "the company's going bankrupt."

Darryl considered that. "Why would it go bankrupt? If they're not paying out claims ..."

"Because no one's paying in anymore," the guy replied. "Why pay your premiums if you won't get you your settlements? Why even buy new policies? Apart from there's no one to process the premiums. Or the new policies. In fact," he stepped around Darryl and handed the counterperson a sheet of paper, "I'm here to cancel my policy."

"Why don't you just hire more people?" Darryl asked the guy behind the counter. "Or reassign your sales force?" Why should he be the only one to be reassigned, to be demoted.

"They're 'working on it'," the man laughed again. Bitterly.

Jeezus, Darryl thought. Weren't insurance companies a big chunk of mutual fund investments? Though he wouldn't admit this to anyone, he didn't really understand the stock market and the economy, but if the insurance companies went bankrupt, wouldn't that have some sort of domino effect?

"So are you going to shit or get off the pot?" the guy behind the counter asked, as Darryl hadn't moved.

In fact, what was happening at the insurance companies *did* have a domino effect—even *before* they went bankrupt. (Which, fortunately, happened more slowly than it would have had proof of death not been required for the life insurance claims that eventually started pouring in.)

With claims being processed so inefficiently, people couldn't pay their medical bills (should they have managed to get medical assistance) (and received a bill for same), their car repair bills (which was, of course, more disruptive), or their house repair bills. Soon all their credit cards would be maxed. Then what?

11

Thursday evening, Marcus met with his IntroGen class. Three students showed up.

So, actually, there *had* been a significant change in Marcus' little corner of academia: when the women disappeared, Assholes #1-3 had abruptly stopped coming to class. Which validated his hypothesis as to why they'd enrolled in the first place.

Oddly enough, he discovered the same thing in his two other classes: attendance by the men was down since the women had disappeared. Was it true then that most men came to class merely to hook up? Marcus sighed. He'd gone into teaching to change the world. That was why he initially thought he'd teach elementary school. There's where the real influence, the real power, was. Which meant, he grimaced, that elementary school teachers should be getting paid what university professors were paid. And vice versa. We really have it all backwards, he thought. No doubt because it's mostly women who teach elementary schools.

But he understood the prejudice and didn't want to spend most of his life being on guard against accusations of child molestation, nor did he want to spend his life addressing insinuations about his masculinity or his heterosexuality just because he *wanted* to teach elementary school.

He then thought about teaching high school, but he knew several people who had gone that route, and they were constantly frustrated because of how much time they spent doing 'classroom management' instead of teaching. The problem, they said, was that the students didn't really want to learn. They were teaching to a captive, and therefore hostile, audience.

So, he'd decided to teach at the university level. At that level, he thought, students *chose* to attend. They actually *paid* to do so. More, they would have chosen to study what he was teaching. So they'd have a genuine interest.

But now he wondered if going to university had become just something to do. A way to postpone getting a job. A way to hook up.

Which made him what, some sort of dim-witted party planner?

Still, he had three very smart, very enthusiastic students in IntroGen. And they were eager to talk that Thursday evening, their first class since the disappearance.

"So what kinds of things have we been seeing since the women disappeared?" Marcus had been thinking that while he waited for funding for his big research project, he could enlist his IntroGen class for some groundwork, incorporate them into the team. Short-term effects included men's reactions.

"There's a lot more violence," Ethan said.

"And why do you think that is?" Marcus was genuinely curious to hear their take on the matter.

"It's because there's a lot more anger," Ethan continued, then anticipated, "and that's because the women are gone."

"How—why would that make men angry?"

"They feel gypped. Because they feel *entitled* to women, to sex."

"They equate the two," Marcus summarized. It was the root of—everything.

Ethan nodded. "And so the women's disappearance is a huge injustice, against them, in their eyes."

"I think—" Devon hesitated.

"Yes?"

"I think it's more than that. I had an insight over the summer—it suddenly occurred to me that the men who spend the most time and energy impressing women—you know, pumping iron, fighting, that sort of thing—they're the ones who value women the least. They're the ones using roofies to rape them, smacking them around. It seemed like a paradox, until I realized they aren't trying to impress the women."

Ethan nodded, and Devon continued.

"They're trying to impress the men. With their heterosexuality. You know, so no one will think they were gay."

"Better to be a sociopath than gay," Ethan said dryly. "Go figure."

"And so now that there's only men," Devon resumed, "the need to assert one's heterosexuality has increased. Hugely."

"Ah," Marcus said. "And so, too, the aggression, the violence. Our construction of manhood *is* sociopathic, isn't it," Marcus nodded to Ethan.

"Thing is," Ethan noted, "the more aggressive people become, the more desensitized to it they'll become. Like you said, with watching TV and playing video games. When you see someone being hurt or killed a hundred times a day or, worse, when you yourself go through the motions of hurting or killing someone a hundred times a day, it quickly becomes no big deal."

"You'd think though," Devon suggested, "that if they *actually* hurt or kill—"

"They wouldn't connect kicking someone with causing internal bleeding or brain damage."

Brendan, who had been quiet to that point, spoke. "I don't know if I want to live in this world," he said softly.

Marcus turned to him. "We don't know that it's permanent," he said carefully.

"I know, but ... I know I'm not a kid anymore, but I miss my

Mom. And my sister. Every minute of the day. To think that I might not ever see them again—" he started to tear up.

"It's not childish to love, to feel attachment," Ethan said to him. "Nor is it unmanly. Or maybe it is. Maybe being manly—"

"I know," Brendan said, "it's just that— It's hard enough dealing with the loss. If I have to go around every day being extra-vigilant ... I just don't know if ..."

Suddenly Marcus understood, not just cognitively, but *emotionally*, the radical feminist arguments for separatism.

"Okay, this is good. All of what you're saying. And I encourage you to start writing it down, if you haven't already. It could turn into published papers, or at least published op-eds. But I'd like to talk about doing something more systematic with our observations. Validate them with some hard research."

"You mean surveys? I'm not sure I want to go to these men and ask ... questions." That was Ethan.

"Okay, what *would* you feel comfortable with? Sitting in some protected place, making notes about what you observe? You could prepare some sort of classification system, and keep a record of how many incidents of what behaviours you saw ..."

They planned through the evening, calling up previous research, setting their parameters, phrasing their research questions, talking about methodology ...

12

On Sunday, that first Sunday, Craig went to visit his dad in the senior citizen complex slash nursing home. He did that every Sunday. The man was in pretty good shape, all things considered. No dementia, no incontinence, he just had to use a walker, and Craig's apartment was, therefore, not an option. No elevator for starters.

As soon as Craig opened the door to the foyer, the stench hit him. He froze for one second, paralyzed by guilt. Why hadn't he thought to come on Friday, as soon as— Had *no one* thought to come? How had they all just ... *forgotten?*

He raced down the hallway to his father's room, putting his hand over his mouth and nose. Was it just urine and feces he was smelling or—he didn't want to know.

Around the corner, he saw a pile of bodies, none moving. It looked like two people had fallen out of their wheelchairs—no, no, no, he recognized his father's burgundy cardigan—

"Dad!" Craig knelt to help—his father had obviously fallen trying to manoeuvre past or perhaps trying to help—but it was too late. Two days without water, Craig calculated then. *Over* two days. All three of them were deceased.

He wasn't a trauma specialist, he didn't think about what to do next, he just sat there, for a good hour, crying, holding his father in his arms. His father had died alone. He had died with no one to bear witness, no one to validate his fears, shore up his hopes, no one to celebrate his life, lament his passing.

That's what Sheyenne would have done. She was the nurse assigned to his father, assigned to provide care to his father. And she did. Not only in the sense of seeing to his needs, but in the sense of really providing *care*, really *caring*.

He didn't know how you could *pay* someone to do that, but they did, he and Elaine. And, amazingly enough, they got what they paid for. People like Sheyenne came to care about strangers who became so much more. They cared and they cared until they could care no more, until the job had made them emotionally bankrupt.

And then what did they do? Craig didn't know. Perhaps they hired themselves out as housecleaners. Because houses didn't need emotional investment, houses didn't lose hope, houses didn't fear obliteration. Houses didn't need someone to be there. Not like his father, and thousands like him, had needed someone. To be there. And now that the women were gone, no one was. There.

Eventually, Craig got up, went to his father's room, returned with a blanket, and covered him. He did the same for the other two gentlemen. He called 911, but the line was busy. No surprise, he thought. This must be happening all over the city, all over the country, perhaps all over the world.

He wandered through the building then, just in case, just to make sure. He covered the bodies as he went, clasping each cold hand one last time, whispering them peace. He could give them that much. But it wasn't enough.

Eventually, he came across two other sons, or grandsons, as distraught as he was, one gently washing his father's body, the other still administering CPR.

"He's gone," he said to the latter, as gently as he could. The young man nodded, then stopped and collapsed into the bedside chair, tears streaming down his cheeks. He'd known; he'd just needed someone to give him permission to stop, to let go.

And so when Andrew took the boys went to visit their grandfather, on the second Sunday, he found the building marked off with HazMat tape.

As soon as he saw it, he knew. He slowed the car to a stop in the parking lot. How could he have not thought— Why didn't he think to— It had been a very difficult past two weeks— Still.

"What's that yellow stuff?" Tommy asked, looking at the tape.

"It's— It means it's closed."

"But Grampy!"

"I know, but we can't see him today."

He'd figure it out later. His father was a cold, heartless idiot who thought more about himself and his own troubles than— Still.

Usually, they went out for dinner after their visit with Grampy, but it was a bit early. And, of course, Andrew had no appetite.

"Are we going to The Castle?" Tommy asked. It was his favourite restaurant. The building had been redone as a castle, and there was a knight in shining armour at the door.

"In a bit," Andrew replied. He wanted to just sit first. Get a cup of coffee. Just sit and calm down, he told himself. Relax, everything will be okay. You didn't know. You can't be expected to think of everything.

He pulled into the parking lot beside the coffee shop, considered just leaving Timmy and Tommy in the car—it would be so much easier—then thought the better of it.

Could he leave them at a table while he stood in line? No, he couldn't do that either.

The line was long. The line was slow. Timmy was fussing in his stroller. Tommy was still upset about not seeing Grampy.

"Just a regular coffee, please," he said when he finally got to the front of the line.

The man took forever to get just a regular coffee, seemingly distracted by anything else, everything else, that was happening in the shop. Eventually, he succeeded at his simple task, then set the cup, saucerless, onto the counter, spilling a bit in the process.

No smiling 'Will there be anything else?' was forthcoming.

Not only were men slower, Andrew had been discovering—everything took longer now, going to the grocery store, going to the pharmacy, even this, getting a quick cup of coffee—they were just as happy to tell you to fuck off as ask if you'd like anything else. It was on their faces and in their body language. It was as if they resented doing something, anything, for someone else. Apparently that was a girl thing.

"How much?" Andrew had to ask.

"Six-fifty."

"What?" He was sure it had been three-twenty-five last time he was here. He hadn't known until that moment that coffee was harvested primarily by women. What else, he wondered. Maybe he should be stocking up on things. He sighed. This could be the last time he just stopped somewhere to 'grab a cup of coffee.'

"You deaf?"

"No, I heard you, it's just—" he pulled a ten out of his wallet.

The man grudgingly gave him his change, as if it was his own money he was handing over. Andrew awkwardly got Timmy's stroller turned around, picked up the cup of coffee, then— Every empty table was cluttered with abandoned cups, saucers, plates, leftover muffins, scones, croissants, crumpled napkins ... The guy next in line jostled him, and Andrew quickly spread his arm out to avoid spilling the hot coffee onto Timmy. It spilled instead onto someone who had come up to the counter for a spoon.

"Hey watch it!" the man said harshly. "You gonna pay for this?" he gestured to his now-coffee-stained windbreaker.

"I'm sorry, it wasn't my fault, I—yeah, sure, give me your address and I'll send a cheque," Andrew said wearily. What the fuck was happening with everyone?

He stood waiting, one hand holding his coffee cup, the other gripping Timmy's stroller, Tommy clinging to his leg.

"Give me a pen and paper," the man demanded.

Unfuckingbelievable. Andrew stared at him, then simply set the now mostly empty cup onto the nearest table and walked out.

"*Now* are we going to The Castle?" Tommy whined.

Andrew blinked back tears. Tears of frustration, and anger, fatigue, and grief. He was overwhelmed. And it had been what, just a week? Two?

"Sure." Actually, it was starting to sound like a good idea. They'd get a table, it would be a clean and nicely set table, one of the servers would come and take their order, politely and cheerfully, they'd sit and chat while they waited for someone else to make their dinner, the server would return and set it onto their table, not spilling a thing, and then they'd take their time eating it. And then he'd get the boys whatever they wanted for dessert. And he'd have a cup of coffee. Maybe two. He'd recover. Everything would be okay.

The Castle had been turned into a serve-yourself buffet.

13

On Tuesday, Darryl called a lawyer. He was nothing if not entitled. And if he wasn't going to get his car repairs reimbursed—we're talking about a vintage Camaro here—he'd sue the insurance company. Before it went bankrupt.

Although women had made up almost half of the law students nationwide—a testament to their strength and drive given that one of the frat chants at Yale, the #1 law school in the country, was "No means Yes, Yes means Anal"—they did not make up half of the lawyers. In fact, most women left the profession. Perhaps it had something to do with the expressed preference that they show their legs and wear high heels. Or the fact that despite having the better grades, they'd somehow end up making partner far less often.

Realizing that if he'd persisted in seeking legal assistance by phone, he would have failed completely, Darryl decided to take another long lunch and simply go to the nearest firm. And rather than waiting for a non-existent receptionist to show up, he just started walking the hallways looking for open doors.

"Are you a lawyer?" Darryl stuck his head into the first open doorway.

"Yes, how can I help you?" a balding man in an expensive suit looked up from the work on his desk.

"I'm looking for someone to help me sue an insurance company."

"Come in," he stood up and offered his hand. "I'm Jack Taylor, Lark, Taylor, and Reel."

Darryl shook Jack's hand, then sat in the chair across from his desk.

"What's at issue?" Jack got right to the point.

Encouraged by the man's eagerness, Darryl told him his story.

"I see," Jack said, thinking it over. "We'd have to ask for a retainer, of course ..."

Darryl expected that. "How much?"

"It would take me a couple hours to draw up the papers, and I'm afraid I charge $500 an hour." It would have taken Janine half an hour, at $40 an hour. "But I can get one of the juniors to do it, if that's okay with you. Their fee is only $300 an hour."

"A junior would be fine," Darryl said. Trying not to show surprise at the fee. He didn't want to seem like an idiot.

"All-righty-o," Jack said, standing, ready to shake Darryl's hand again. "If you could just write out a cheque, payable to Lark, Taylor, and Reel, I can get the wheels in motion!"

He didn't say *when* he could get the wheels in motion. Almost all of their juniors, as well as their paralegals and legal assistants, had been women.

As it turned out, that didn't really matter. Because most of the court clerks had also been women. So even if they'd been able to draw up the papers, they wouldn't have been able to file them for a while. Two years. Maybe three. Or four. The wheels of justice had turned slowly even *before* the women's disappearance. Now they were pretty much mired in mud.

Darryl wrote the cheque.

14

As a sensitive, studious young man, James was all too happy not to have to go back to school, and all too capable of keeping up with his schoolwork on his own.

Not that it would lead to where he'd hoped. Universities were still open, yes, but it was just a matter of time. With half as many applicants to fill their first year classes, many faculties, perhaps even many universities, would close. Of course, they could lower their standards to keep their numbers up, but then where would they get all the remedial instructors they'd need?

James was good with Timmy and Tommy. He read out loud to them, giving each of the characters a different voice, and using his hands to dramatize the events. Diane had done that, Andrew realized, missing her. He hadn't had time to miss her, he told himself. That's why he hadn't thought much about her until now. James was also patient with the boys. Far more patient than he, Andrew, had ever been.

Early in the second week, when the bruising of his ribs had subsided—they decided they were just bruised, not broken—James had been confident enough to take the kids to the library. It was quite an outing, apparently. Timmy and Tommy had much to tell Andrew that night.

"We got lots of books, Daddy!" Tommy took Andrew's hand and showed him the pile in the corner of the room. Andrew recognized *Curious George* at once.

"Lots books!" Timmy confirmed, hurrying after them.

Andrew didn't have a spare room for James. He wished he did. He'd love for James to live in. But, so, they'd designated a corner of the living room as his. In fact, he and the boys had built a fort in that corner. And though it was James' fort, his quiet place, Andrew saw that the boys were often inside. James didn't seem to mind. Andrew certainly didn't.

"And we almost got a fish!"

Andrew looked at James, questioning.

"The library has a fish tank in the kids' area. We asked one if it wanted to come home with us."

"But it said it was happy where it was. IN THE WATER!" Tommy crowed and started laughing uproariously.

James started laughing too, but then quickly put his hand on his side. Andrew wasn't sure he got the joke.

Turned out to be a good thing they'd signed out the maximum number of books. The library was closed day after. Couldn't stay open with just 15% of their usual staff.

That evening, Andrew saw James reading a book about child development. My god but he should give the kid a raise.

"So," Andrew said cheerily to James, sipping his coffee that Friday morning while the boys ate their breakfast, a breakfast James had prepared, "you're okay with all this? It's been a week—well a little over a week … I think you've done a super job, and I hope you want to carry on."

"I do," James replied. The last week and a half had been great. In fact, he'd been hoping that maybe he could become a live-in nanny or whatever, but …

"Okay, then, shall we say that every second Friday is pay day?" Andrew got up, opened the drawer of the small table in the hallway that served as a desk of sorts, and took out his chequebook.

"Um," James said, "I don't have a bank account."

"Oh." Of course not. The boy was only what, fourteen? This was probably his first job. "Okay, how about we go to the bank today on my lunch break and open one up for you?"

"Okay. So …"

"I'll swing by at noon, and we'll drive over to the one at the plaza, is that okay?"

"Yeah, I guess. I mean, I don't know. Is that bank a good one?"

"Banks are banks," Andrew said. "I don't think there's much difference from one to another."

"Okay then. We'll be ready. Thank you," he added.

Andrew had only forty-five minutes for lunch and it would take half an hour just to drive back home, pick up James and the boys, then drive to the bank. But when else was he supposed to do stuff like this? It occurred to him that Diane had dealt with anything that had to be dealt with during business hours. Taking the car to the shop, the kids to the dentist—the dentist! He should check the calendar to see if they had any appointments coming up. Diane would have written them on the calendar. And did he have to take Timmy to the doctor? At what age did kids finish getting all their vaccinations? He had no idea.

James was waiting out front with Timmy in the stroller and Tommy beside him, holding onto his hand.

"In you go!" Andrew said as he opened the back door and Tommy climbed in and across into his car seat. Then he lifted Timmy in, secured them both, folded up the stroller, and put it in the trunk. James got in the front, and Andrew got behind the wheel again.

As soon as they pulled in to the plaza, they saw the long line. Two long lines. And a cluster at the door. The latter probably consisting of those feeling too special to wait in line.

"Wait here a minute," Andrew said to James, then went to inquire.

"Is this a line for the tellers?" he asked a tall, curly-haired man standing in one of the lines.

"No, this one goes to the Loans Officer."

"Oh." Andrew was surprised. All of these men were applying for a loan?

"I've got enough to get by for a month or so," the man offered, "but I'm thinking the bank has only so much in reserve. What if there's nothing left if and when I *do* need a loan, you know?"

"Right," Andrew said vaguely. He hadn't thought about that. But now that he did … "They'd be tapped out that quickly?"

"Do the math. Half of their clients are suddenly gone, so they're not making any more deposits. And half of those who are left—all the guys with kids who've had to quit their jobs or who've been laid off—they're suddenly unemployed. So not only are *they* not making deposits, they need something to pay their rent with, so …"

"Right," Andrew said again.

"Also, ya gotta figure profits are going to be down, what with things being such a mess at the moment, so *businesses* will be making lower deposits, so *they* may be coming for loans as well …" The man ran his fingers through his hair.

Maybe, Andrew thought, he should apply for a loan now too. Or at least withdraw all of his money, before they put a limit on how much you could withdraw. Didn't that happen in a recession or a depression or whatever? No, if things got that bad, paper money would become worthless, wouldn't it?

On the other hand, IT was primarily male, so online banking would probably continue to be okay, so if he left his money in his account, he'd be able to keep making payments on his credit cards. So they wouldn't be cancelled. But maybe he should apply for new, extra credit cards now. Just to be on the safe side.

He went back to his car.

"I don't have to open up an account today," James had rolled down his window.

"Actually," Andrew got back into the car, "I'm wondering whether you should open up an account at all," Andrew said. "I mean, maybe you should just wait until things get back to normal."

"You think they ever will? Get back to normal?"

Andrew thought about that. And realized that he hoped not. He'd come to see that a few things were seriously wrong with normal. More than a few things. For example, and this seemed to come out of nowhere, why wasn't Sharon a Project Manager? She'd *trained* him for godsake. And she was his *assistant*? She was *his* assistant? It didn't make any sense. Truth be told, she didn't just format his reports to make them all pretty, she made several helpful suggestions as to what to include. In fact, some of the recommendations in that last report had been hers. Three, in fact. Of the five.

"I don't know," Andrew finally said, staring out the windshield.

Then he turned to James. "You miss your mom?"

James nodded. "She was going to leave. My dad."

Andrew wasn't surprised.

"But I don't think that's what happened."

"No," Andrew agreed. They both stared out the windshield.

After a few moments, Andrew returned to the issue at hand. "'Course, once you've got an account, you could always make deposits and withdrawals at the ATM."

James imagined being mugged at an ATM and having all his money taken.

"Or you can just pay me in cash," he said, "and I can keep it at your place. You can be my ATM," he smiled hopefully.

"Yeah, maybe that's best. Okay, give me a few more minutes," he glanced into the back seat, "and I'll go make a withdrawal now."

The line at the ATM wasn't nearly as long as the other two.

"No problem, we're good, aren't we?" James said to Tommy in the back seat.

"Yup, we're good!" Tommy cheerfully mimicked James.

Fifteen minutes later, Andrew got into the car and handed Andrew a wad of cash. "I'll have to give you the rest next week," he said apologetically. He hadn't done the math: the limit for withdrawals at the ATM was lower than James' wages for the week. He hoped the ATMs didn't break down. Though there was no reason why they should. Surely the people who kept them working and filled with cash were men, like the Brinks' truck guys.

"No problem," James said, tucking the money into his wallet, then returning it to the buttoned pocket of his pants.

Andrew saw Richard at Reception as he rounded the corner. "I had to take my—" Nanny? Babysitter? They were both demeaning to James in some vague way that he couldn't quite put his finger on. In any case, Household Assistant was more accurate, given everything he was doing …

He heard himself apologize then to Richard for the long lunch he'd taken, smiling excessively as he did so. It was humiliating. He'd never apologized before to Richard for taking a long lunch. Or smiled like that.

Turned out the tall, curly-haired guy was pretty close to the mark.

The banks were able to deal with, or, at least within a week or two, recover from, the sudden loss of almost all of their tellers and many of their loan officers.

But yes, they did limit their loans. Because deposits *were* down. More than 50%. And their reserves *were* limited.

15

While they'd been sitting in the car, Elliot was on his way back to the hospital.

He'd been fired the week before. Most of the fathers who'd been in Peds and the NICU those first few days had been fired. Because look, if you've got a job, you can't just not show up when your kid is sick.

It hadn't mattered to any of them. Because they hadn't gotten the bill. And, well, because their kids hadn't made it.

Losing his kid the way he had, getting fired—

It was enough to make Elliot get a gun and blow his brains out.

But not before he went back to the hospital and put a bullet into every doctor he could find.

Including Dr. Harrison.

16

A week had gone by and Darryl still hadn't heard anything from his lawyer. Suspecting legal incompetence, his next move was going to be a visit to City Hall. However, since he passed his MP's office on the way, he figured what the hell, go right to the top.

He opened the door and was pleased to see that the large room was full of eager, competent young men sitting at various desks and tables, answering phones, preparing mail-outs, whatever. At least his rep, Donald Ellis, was unfazed by the disappearance of the women. Nothing had changed. His campaign for re-election was going full steam ahead.

One of the young men immediately came to the counter.

"Hello, may I help you?"

"Yes, I'd like to talk to my MP about something," Darryl paused, not quite sure how to proceed, "and I'm hoping for his assistance or intervention or—"

"Certainly, I understand," the young man said brightly. "Unfortunately, Mr. Ellis is at a meeting at the moment, but I'm authorized to meet with you and take down the details, if you'd like."

"Sure, okay."

"This way please." The young man led Darryl to a corner desk and gestured for him to have a seat. He then picked up a pen, set a notepad in front of him, and prepared to listen. Darryl was impressed. He gave him the whole story, from the collision on the road, to the failure of his insurance company to respond to his satisfaction, to the apparent inability of the lawyer he'd spoken to. The young man nodded throughout and made notes.

"I just think," Darryl concluded, "that the government should be doing something about the situation. Something that would make sure the insurance companies continued to pay out claims—"

"Of course," the young man nodded and kept writing.

"Or see that the legal system keeps working. I mean there's no reason things should fall apart just because there aren't any more women around, right?"

"Of course," the young man nodded and kept writing. He looked up and saw that Darryl seemed finished.

"Thank you for coming in," he stood, and reached out to shake Darryl's hand. "I can assure you that we will definitely look into this, sir."

'Sir.' Darryl liked that. A little respect, yes.

After Darryl left, the young man neatly folded his sheet of notes, then slid it into the slot of the suggestion box in the corner. Where it stayed.

Darryl was right. Nothing had changed.

Or so he thought.

Briefing materials weren't being prepared. So MPs weren't prepared. For anything.

Public relations weren't being managed quite as comprehensively. So MPs looked bad.

Thank you letters didn't get sent. Relationships became strained.

Emails didn't get answered. Constituents become unsupportive.

Important international meetings had to be cancelled for lack of translators.

Formal functions at all levels became sloppy, and the energetic enthusiasm that fuelled the back-slapping and back-scratching seeped away little by little. Men did start filling those event planning positions, but they just weren't as organized. It turned out they weren't as detail-oriented as women. At all levels and in almost all contexts. Preparing blueprints seemed to be the only exception.

The organization that made so many men's productive lives possible had been due, one way or another, to women. Take a look at any man *without* a fleet of women behind him. He flounders and bullshits his way until some woman, still deluded by ... everything, takes pity on him. Or some other woman gets annoyed enough, by him, by everything, to just do it herself. As in the home, so too in the office.

17

Midweek, as Andrew was unlocking his door, the old guy on whose door he'd knocked when he was looking for someone to look after his kids stopped him.

"My cheque didn't come."

"What?" Andrew was tired. He was always tired at the end of the work day. Far more tired than he used to be.

"My government cheque. It didn't come."

"Oh." Right. "It might just be delayed, given," Andrew said, then smiled, hoping to step inside and close his door.

"What?" The man cupped his hand to his ear.

"It might be delayed," Andrew spoke up. "The post office is probably overloaded. I imagine most of the sorters were women."

"What?"

Andrew sighed. He didn't have time for this.

"If I don't get my cheque, I can't pay my rent," the man whined. "The super's going to kick me out."

"He wouldn't do that," Andrew assured him. Knowing full well the super would do exactly that.

"Where am I going to live?" The man clutched Andrew's arm.

"Don't you have a son or daughter ..." Someone *else* who can deal with this?

"My daughter, she didn't come last week. I think something's happened to her. I keep calling her, and she says leave a message, she'll call back, but she never does. I think something's happened to her."

Oh god. He doesn't know. Of course he wouldn't. He probably never leaves his apartment. Knows only what's on TV. And the goddamn news was … useless. Still.

"Can you find out what happened to my cheque?" the man begged him.

Actually, Andrew thought maybe he could. If the government had any brains at all, they would have changed over to direct deposit immediately.

"Sure," he relented, no doubt moved by guilt and the need to atone for neglecting his own father. "Come on in, and let's see."

"Daddy!" Tommy ran to him and grabbed him around the legs.

Timmy was right behind. "Daddy home!"

"Hey, how was your day?" Andrew was going to pick them up one at a time and give them a whirl, but instead Tommy took his hand and pulled him into the living room.

"Daddy, come look! We made art!" He pointed to the floor. To an intriguing Lego sculpture.

"Cool!" Andrew said.

"Ducks!" Timmy shouted.

Andrew turned back to Tommy. It was supposed to be ducks?

"James took us to the park," he explained. "We saw the ducks."

"Ah."

He turned back to the man lingering at the doorway.

"Come in and have a seat, Mr.— I'm sorry, I don't know your name."

"What?"

"I don't know your name!" he shouted.

"Mr. Begonia," James said, coming out of the kitchen, tea towel in hand. "Hi," he nodded to the man.

"You know him?"

"I know his name. He lives in our hall, right?"

"Right. He didn't get his government cheque, and if he doesn't pay rent, he says the super will evict him."

"He's probably right," James said. "The super's a real asshole."

"Well, I told him I'd try to help. His daughter hasn't been by— He doesn't even know …"

They helped Mr. Begonia into one of the chairs at the kitchen table, and Andrew pulled his laptop across the table toward him. Since Andrew was no longer a Project Manager, he didn't really need to be taking his laptop to work every day, so he'd been leaving it at home for James, who was working his way through his high school courses at an impressive pace.

"Hang on," James leaned in, saved his work, and minimized the window. Andrew quickly found the government website and, yes, all recipients of pension cheques were being encouraged to change immediately to direct deposit. A 'stop payment' had been issued on all cheques not cashed within ten days of delivery, and all future payments would be made by direct deposit only.

"You can get your cheque by direct deposit," Andrew said to Mr. Begonia.

"What?"

"That's pretty stupid," James observed, reading the announcement over Andrew's shoulder. "Most pensioners probably don't even have a computer, let alone know how to use one. So how would they find out about this?"

"Good point."

"Can you get my cheque?"

"No," Andrew turned to him. "You need to set up direct deposit."

"What?" The man leaned forward toward Andrew.

"You need to arrange for your cheques to be deposited directly into the bank!"

"Oh, my daughter said I should do that, but I don't trust computers."

"I don't think you have much choice now," Andrew said. Just as well. He imagined Mr. Begonia going to the bank … "The post office is closed." There. That should make things easier.

"Oh. Okay, then." He sat there, nodding his head.

Andrew waited.

"How do I do that? I go to the bank to do that? Can you take me to the bank to do that?"

"Couldn't we just do it for him?" James said quickly, seeing Andrew become increasingly frustrated. "If he's already got an account … He just needs to establish online access to it, right? Then, what, send the government his account number?"

Andrew sighed. "Yeah. But he's still not going to get his cheque in time. I guess I could pay this month's rent for him. I'm sure he'll pay me back," he said uncertainly. Mr. Begonia probably wouldn't even know, or remember …

"Can you get my cheque for me?" Mr. Begonia tried to get up.

"I'm going to set up direct deposit for you, and then you can just write your rent cheques to the super like usual."

"What?"

"I need a blank cheque," he said more loudly. "Your cheque book?"

"I'll get it," James said. "Hey, Tommy, wanna come with me for a scavenger hunt?"

"Okay!" Tommy beamed and went with James into the hall. Sure enough, Mr. Begonia had left his door open. They went inside, James looked in all the obvious places, telling Tommy to look under the couch, then behind the chair, and they returned with Mr. Begonia's cheque book. And his wallet.

"In case you need his social insurance number or something," he said, handing it to Andrew.

"Good thinking."

Andrew went to the website of Mr. Begonia's bank and started to set up online banking for him.

"What's your daughter's name?" Andrew asked him.

"What?"

"Your daughter's name. That will be your password."

"Constance."

"Thank god it's at least seven letters long," Andrew muttered.

Then he went back to the government site and set up direct deposit for his pension cheques.

"When's she coming back?"

"Who?"

"Constance!"

"Oh. Um, I don't know." He handed the cheque book and the wallet back to James.

"Maybe you should keep one of the cheques," James said. "Once the money's in his account, you can pay yourself back with it. Just fill it out and ask him to sign it."

"Good idea." He tore off a cheque and tucked it into his own wallet.

"The meals-on-wheels lady didn't come either," Mr. Begonia said. "She comes every week with seven dinners and puts them in my freezer. She's a nice lady. I can't remember if she came last week, but she must have because I have one meal left. But sometimes I forget to eat … She didn't come today."

Andrew thought for a second, then sighed. "That's because the women are gone."

"What?"

"The women are gone!"

"What women?"

"All the women!"

"Maybe you shouldn't've told him that," James said.

"I know," Andrew said, looking anxiously at Mr. Begonia, "but otherwise he's going to keep thinking something has happened to his daughter."

"Something has."

"Yeah, but—"

"My daughter too? She's gone?"

Andrew nodded.

"But she's okay?"

Andrew and James glanced at each other. Andrew sighed again. "Yes, she's okay."

"So she'll come next week? And the meals-on-wheels lady?"

Andrew thought about lending him grocery money, since he couldn't imagine him going to the ATM, but he couldn't imagine him going to the grocery store either. He certainly couldn't imagine him trying to make himself dinner.

"We could just invite him here for dinner every day," James said. "I can make extra."

"Are you sure? It's not exactly in your job description."

James shrugged. "What else can we do?"

Andrew agreed. The man apparently didn't eat that much. Not if he had one meal left. It had been almost three weeks.

"Okay." It really was the easiest solution. And James definitely deserved a raise.

18

That Thursday, Marcus walked into class to find Ethan with a black eye.

"What happened?" he peered closely at the injury.

"Oh, you know …"

"You're okay? Did you have it looked at?"

"Yes. No. Where does one go to 'have it looked at' these days?"

Devon, who was already there as well, nodded, then started to take out his laptop, texts, notebook, and pen … all so very slowly. Marcus eventually realized that he was using just the one hand. His left hand.

"You too?"

"Yeah." He held up his bruised right hand.

"Either of you know where Brendan is?" Marcus asked, glancing toward the door. "He's not usually late …"

"Um," Ethan looked at Devon, who returned the look, "Brendan won't be coming."

"He—" Devon couldn't say it. "Remember when he said—" he tried again.

"He slit his wrists."

Suddenly light-headed, Marcus sat down in the nearest desk. "But …"

"We found him on the weekend," Ethan continued, "when we went over to work on our project."

"But …"

"There was nothing to be done," Devon added.

Even if an ambulance *had* responded to their 911 call.

"I'm sorry," Ethan said. "We thought you'd know."

"No, I …" Women managed the communications, and— He was distracted by the sudden thought that given that they did, they could've just— No, women were as likely as men to demand their baby girls be in pink and their boys be in blue …

"No," Marcus tried again, "intra-university communications seem to have … failed."

He failed. He should've known. Should've anticipated. He should've talked to Brendan. He should've—

"We called his father," Devon offered.

"He's not doing so well either," Ethan added. "First his wife and daughter. And now—"

Marcus tried to take it all in. Eventually he caught up. Sort of.

"And you two? Are you— How are you—"

"There's been a fair amount of moving around in the dorm," Ethan said. "Some of the guys—like me and Devon—have moved in together …"

"Banded together," Devon called it what it was.

"We're making sure no one's alone …"

"Alone with a thug for a roommate."

"So …" Marcus floundered a bit, hands on the desk, facing them, wondering whether he should ask about the research they'd planned to do. Wondering whether he should instead jump over this to Stoltenberg and Jensen. Wondering whether they should just talk first …

"It's crazy out there." Ethan said. "It's like some contagion …"

Devon nodded. "A sociocultural contagion. And everyone's rabid."

"It was bad enough before, having to always be … aware. Because I'm gay. But now …"

"But I'm *not* gay!" Devon insisted, then backtracked. "I—I just meant to say that—"

Ethan grinned at him and let him struggle.

"I just meant they're not targeting just gays anymore. They're targeting whoever—whoever—"

"Whoever they think isn't a *real* man."

"Right."

"And you're either a real man or you're a fag," Ethan said. "There's no in between available for people like you who are straight, but not sociopathic."

Well put, Marcus thought.

Remembering one of his girlfriends, Devon had a thought. "Just like there's no in between—there *wasn't* an in between," he corrected himself, "for women. I mean, a straight woman couldn't just want sex. If she did, she was a slut. Case closed."

Marcus nodded. "The virgin-whore thing."

"The virgin-whore-dyke thing," Ethan clarified. "Because if she doesn't have sex, if she doesn't *want* to have sex, she's more likely to be called a dyke. Than seen as a pure woman waiting for marriage or some such."

"So, actually, it's not quite the same," Marcus ventured. "It's just as constricting, but it's not a 'real woman' or 'homosexual' dichotomy."

"Unless a 'real woman' is defined as a slut."

"Or a virgin."

They thought about that. It seemed kind of right. Yet so incredibly wrong.

"Regardless," Ethan said, turning to Devon, "even though you're not gay, you're being penalized, *assaulted*, for not performing masculinity."

Devon nodded.

"And the thing you have to ask," Ethan continued, "is 'Why?' I mean, is it just because simple minds can't handle a spectrum? It has to be either/or?"

"Don't think so," Devon shook his head. "Many of these guys are smart. Or at least smart enough."

"Regardless, why would you beat someone up just because they don't fit your either/or, just because you consider them some sort of freak?"

They wondered about that for a few moments.

"Because beating someone up is your response to everything," Devon blurted out, then laughed. "It's not really funny, but—"

"But we do encourage, and condone, violence," Marcus agreed, at least in part, with Devon's explanation. "In males."

Ethan nodded. "And we *don't* encourage self-control."

"You're right," Devon said. "'*Real* men' are those who *lose* control, who get angry, who fly into a rage."

Marcus nodded. "Girls are taught to be patient. Boys are taught that if they shout and run around and wreck stuff, they get what they want."

He had a new thought then. "The prerequisite for self-control is self-awareness, and the prerequisite for self-awareness is introspection. And introspection—thinking about our inner states, our feelings, our motivations— Is that just another thing girls are taught to do and boys not? Or is it something men simply *can't* do? At least not as well as women."

"But wait a minute," Devon backed up. "Isn't being a man being about being *in* control?" He thought about all the upper stiff lip shit. "So there's a contradiction ..." No surprise.

"Maybe it's about being in control of your emotions," Ethan said. "Your *softer* emotions," Ethan qualified. "The ones that might get in the way of aggression."

"Regardless ..." Devon trailed off into the silence that followed.

"What if it's not, or not just, sociocultural?" Ethan suggested a few moments later. "The violence. I mean, they feed growth hormones to the animals that a lot of people eat … What if most of the men walking around have excessively high levels of testosterone?"

"Guys who take steroids are super aggressive," Devon noted. "Steroids are testosterone, aren't they?"

"I once read about a guy who had a pituitary tumour that meant his brain didn't produce testosterone, and he reported no urge to be violent. When he started receiving testosterone injections, he started to feel such an urge."

"The evidence *is* out there, isn't it," Marcus noted, thinking. "But not only does testosterone increase violence, violence increases testosterone. They've done studies. Before and after playing football, I think it was."

"So it's a cause as well as an effect—a feedback loop. Great." Ethan grimaced.

"So what are we saying," Devon asked after a moment. "That most men today are suffering from testosterone poisoning?"

Marcus stared at them. His first thought was that it was a brilliant hypothesis. They hadn't used growth hormones when he was growing up … What if that *was* a factor?

His second thought was that they might not stay alive long enough to test the hypothesis.

They decided to revamp their research project, abandon the methodology they'd decided on. It looked like they would be better off just keeping thoughtful, thorough journals. Personal records. Subjective accounts.

Marcus suddenly realized why so much of women's 'evidence' was just that. Personal records. Subjective accounts. And, therefore, doomed to be dismissed, rejected, *as* personal, subjective. Anecdotal.

But what choice did they have? The disemp—the *un*empowered couldn't *do* 'real' research. Either they had no access to the channels or it was simply too great of a risk. If not physically, certainly professionally.

"Okay," Marcus rose, almost three hours later. A good three hours. They'd gotten into Stoltenberg and Jensen after all. "Till next week?" It was a hope. A prayer, if Marcus hadn't been an atheist.

"Next week," the two of them echoed, then headed toward the door.

"Wait!" Marcus called out after them. "Let me give you a ride to—the shuttle stop? No, let me give you a ride right to your dorm door."

On the way out to the parking lot, Ethan said, in a fake-casual way, "I've decided to get a gun."

Silence. A protracted silence.

Finally Marcus spoke. "Do you know someone who can show you how to use it? Safely?"

19

Justin was one of hundreds, thousands, of young men who were laid off. Things were in such disarray— With half the population gone, there was a significant decline in demand. There was also a failure to properly manage the remaining demand—by making sales, by acquiring and keeping new clients … As long as revenue was down, expenses had to be cut, people had to be let go. Last in, first out.

They say that everyone should have enough savings to get by for six months in the event of a layoff, but, Justin thought, whoever said that must've been thinking of people with six-figure salaries. He'd been making $60,000, but only for the last couple years. He was only twenty-six and had just gotten his MBA, at twenty-four. He'd been hoping to land a position that paid considerably more than $60,000, but when reality set in, he felt lucky to have landed any position at all that actually required his MBA. Problem was, he had close to $30,000 in student debt. And since he'd been supporting his wife and a six-year-old, he was lucky to be breaking even. Which meant that when he was laid off, he had nothing in reserve.

He cancelled the lease on his car immediately and started using the bus. He also cancelled his little-used membership at a golf club and sold what he could—his golf clubs, then his skis and his skates, and then his entertainment system, and even, eventually, his old iPods. But every other young man, it seemed, was doing the same, and he didn't get much for any of it. He should've. Given.

But he couldn't lose the apartment. His parents lived clear across the country and, in any case, going back home had to be a last resort. A very last resort.

So he also applied for a loan. Ended up having to wait in line for ten hours. To make an appointment six months hence. No telling whether his application would be approved. No telling when, or even if, the money would appear.

He started making cold calls. No one was hiring a freshly minted MBA.

He studied the classifieds. There were tons of jobs. For receptionists, secretaries, file clerks, tellers, nurses, daycare teachers, elementary school teachers, and high school teachers. He wasn't qualified for any of those positions.

Maybe he could be someone's executive assistant, he'd thought, but he didn't see any ads for EAs. He suspected that whatever EA positions there had been had gone straight to someone's relative or friend or friend of a friend. Nothing new there. He'd tell his friends about jobs he knew about too. Come to think of it, all of the jobs he'd had had been acquired as a result of his connections. Problem was, his connections were in male-dominated fields. Or at least for positions typically filled by men. It seemed impossible to cross over to the other side. Which meant, of course, that as long as cronyism ruled the day, that day would continue to be divided by gender.

Suck it up, he thought to himself, and called about the receptionist, secretary, file clerk, and teller positions. He was shocked to discover they paid little more than minimum wage. Some paid as little as four-fifty a week. He couldn't support a kid on that!

Then an ad for EXOTIC DANCERS!!! caught his eye. Five hundred a night. Seriously? He actually considered it.

He had better things to do with his time than spend four hours a day working out, but he wasn't in bad shape and he'd always thought of himself as a good dancer. And, truth be told, the women he'd seen at the clubs he'd gone to—it was standard operating procedure for business lunch meetings—hadn't been exactly Janet Jackson.

He'd recently discovered Janet Jackson because "without fresh meat", as the VJ had said with a grin, they were raiding the archives and airing videos by Janet Jackson, Paula Abdul, and a bunch of others he'd never seen before. Pity, he'd thought. They were pretty hot.

So he called the place, Grinders, and received an automated message saying that interested applicants should attend the orientation session being held that very night.

He left Liam with a neighbour and went to check it out.

What he discovered shouldn't have surprised him that much. Now that the women were gone, drag queen shows had become popular with straight audiences. Not ones to miss an opportunity that was staring them in the face, some of the younger performers added more dance to their song-and-dance routines, and then very quickly starting doing just the dance.

Club managers hired them immediately to occupy their suddenly empty stages. To fill their suddenly empty tills. So suddenly there weren't enough drag queens. Ads were placed and overnight all of the drag queens had classes. Full classes.

Justin found himself in one such class. At first, when he realized that he wouldn't be dancing as a man—why he'd thought he would be, he had no idea—he started to leave. He wasn't gay. There was no way he was getting into a dress, putting on make-up … But a quick glance around the room told him he wasn't the only one. He wasn't the only one who wasn't gay and he wasn't the only one whose hopes of climbing the corporate ladder had disappeared overnight. And he wasn't the only one to recognize the realities of supply and demand and to want to be ahead of the curve. If he waited until his money completely ran out, he might not have even this stupid opportunity. Little did he know about this particular demand.

And he wasn't the only one with a kid to support.

So he learned how to move as if his center of gravity was in his hips rather than in his shoulders. He learned how to use his hands, to be expressive with his hands. He learned how to use his face, to be expressive with his face.

He learned how to put on make-up. And a wig. And stockings.

He learned, tried to learn, how to walk in heels.

He learned what it feels like to have the hair ripped off his entire body.

He drew the line at implants. T & A implants, their queen of queens, DeVonn, called them. Apparently the process was painful, and expensive, but, he said, worth it. As was a little face work here and there. Some even had the facial reconstruction surgery that transgenders had been getting for years. Apparently there was no shortage of surgeons with assistants to perform those procedures.

Good thing, because once a new standard was set, you had to meet that standard if you wanted to stay in business. Tension between the 'real' trannies and the 'opportunists' developed. It was harsh. But who cared? Certainly not the men in the audience.

Friday night, Arnie pulled in, as he did every Friday. He was aching for things to be back the way they were, because everything had been just fine the way it was, why did the women have to go and wreck everything? That Friday night, Justin was making his debut. He was waiting in the wings, ready. Or not.

"Wait a minute!" The manager grabbed Justin away from the stage and pointed to his feet. "You can't go on like that, are you crazy?"

Justin's blistered toes had started bleeding again, so he'd bandaged them up before putting on the stockings, and then the open-toed, high-heeled, slingbacks he was supposed to wear. "You think that's *sexy?* Take off those bandages!"

"You want me to bleed all over the stage?"

"Good question. No. Next!"

Justin was afraid that if he didn't perform, he wouldn't get paid. "So let me wear regular shoes!" Shoes that didn't make your toes bleed. Shoes you could actually walk in. Maybe even dance in.

"What, you wanna wear your Nikes on stage?" The man shoved Justin aside.

"Here," DeVonn thrust a pair of high-heeled boots into Justin's hands. "Put these on."

Justin nodded his thanks and quickly, painfully, changed his footwear, then stood in the wings again, waiting.

Of course he was nervous. And of course he felt like an idiot. It wasn't in his nature to put himself on display like this, to preen and prance—to be entertainment.

But he tried. For Liam. He could make more in one night here than he could in a whole week at a call center. Which was the only job for which he'd received an interview. And the best part was that Liam could be here with him. Many of the dancers had kids, and they all brought them to the club. They'd even set up a designated kids' corner and filled it with make-up and costumes no longer stage worthy. The kids had fun and mostly stayed out of their way. When someone was on stage, he didn't have to worry about his kid; someone else would be looking after him, looking out for him. They were all in the same bind, so they became each other's family in a way. In the way circus performers became family, Justin thought.

The music started, a stupid bump-and-grind, and Justin made his slow and seductive (he hoped) way onto the stage. He felt stupid. So stupid, moving the way he was moving. A pole had been lowered from the rafters; yes, he was actually doing a pole dance for part of his number.

The hoots and hollers caught him off guard. He knew the men did that—he'd done it himself on numerous occasions—but from his perspective, now, it didn't sound like they were cheering so much as—

"That's it, baby!" Someone whistled.

"Show me what you got!"

"Bend over for me baby, show me your hole!"

That one made him stumble. He had never been that—crude? That clear?

He recovered and resumed his routine. He strutted across the stage, stopped to pose with his finger in his mouth—and felt like a *complete* idiot. Grown men do not put their fingers in their mouths. Then he made his way toward the pole, around and around, closer and closer. Then he hefted himself up, thinking of it as a sort of vertical pommel horse ...

And then he fell off. Sort of. Forgetting he had high-heeled boots on, he lost his balance when he landed and fell over. The men in the audience laughed, some of them until they had tears in their eyes. It was humiliating.

He ran off the stage. Or would have if he'd been able to run in heels.

"It's okay, Justin," DeVonn said to him. "Takes a while. You did good."

He was embarrassed at how much that meant. For her—him—to comfort him, reassure him.

"Now go and mingle, like we're supposed to."

Right. In between numbers, they were supposed to double as waiters—waitresses—serving drinks. He collected himself, shrugged it off, and headed out. He could do this.

"Come over here, sugar, come sit on my lap," a man with a crew cut called out to him. "Do you think you can do that without falling off?" he guffawed and everyone around him laughed along.

Justin just glared at him.

"Come on, sugar, give it a try!" the man waved a hundred dollar bill.

Okay, that stopped him. They hadn't been told about this though. Justin glanced at DeVonn, who nodded for him to go ahead. The manager was also telling him to go ahead already, impatiently gesturing with his hands.

So Justin awkwardly sat on the man's lap. Oh god, he felt like an idiot. He felt four years old. Adults do not sit in other people's laps.

"Oh, you're a bit of a dead fish, aren't you," the man said after a few seconds. "Can't you move around a little bit?"

Justin looked helplessly at DeVonn again, who swung her, his, hips in a circle. Justin started moving around a bit.

"That's it, sugar, now you're getting it."

God, the man was so patronizing. Justin tried to remember how long lap dances were. He'd had one or two himself, but couldn't remember, truthfully, how long—

"Lick it," the man was saying. Ordering, actually.

What?

He was dangling the hundred dollar bill in front of Justin's mouth. "Lick it for papa," he repeated.

Justin stuck out his tongue and touched the bill. Just a bit. God knows where it had been.

"You call that a lick? I said LICK IT!" the man was angry. "Don't you know how to use that mouth of yours?"

Justin tried again. He licked the bill a little bit more.

"Oh get off me, bitch," he man shoved Justin off of him, and bouncers quickly moved in. Patrons weren't allowed to touch them, Justin remembered that much. "You're makin' me lose my steel!"

At the end of the night, Justin joined the others at the bar. Payment in cash, that was the deal, end of each night. But when the manager got to Justin, he just laughed at him.

"Five hundred," Justin said with as much dignity as he had left, and held out his hand.

The manager laughed harder. "Five hundred? Five hundred is your maximum earning potential. You *start* at *one* hundred!"

What? The ad had said five hundred.

"But the ad—"

"Are you calling me a liar?" the manager challenged.

DeVonn sent Justin a look.

"No, I—"

"And honey, for your performance tonight, you don't even get that!"

"You can't do that!" Justin protested. "I—"

"I can and I just did," the manager said. "Tell you what though. Just to show you what a nice guy I am, you can come back tomorrow night and try again."

Justin gaped, as the man just turned and walked away.

Unfuckingbelievable, he thought, as he lit a cigarette with shaking hands once he was outside the back door, Liam at his side. He'd been attending those stupid classes all fucking week, he'd done his best, he'd done six fucking dances, and served drinks for four fucking hours, tottering on those damn boots, getting leered at and jeered at, and now he didn't even get paid? Not five hundred, not even one hundred? He blinked back the tears that had been forming, even more angry that this was reducing him to tears.

"Hey sugar, I'll give you a chance to make it up to me, what do you say?" It was Mr. Asshole. Justin recognized the voice. He grabbed Liam's hand.

"One hundred?" the man held out the hundred dollar bill again.

"For what?" Justin said stupidly.

"For what," the man repeated as he stared out into space, incredulous at Justin's stupidity. He turned back to Justin and shouted, "What do you think?" He was already undoing his zipper.

Justin recoiled. Then reconsidered.

"Go back inside, Liam, okay? Daddy'll be there in a minute," he gently pushed Liam back inside.

Sometimes, you just do what you gotta to do, he told himself. Besides, if some guy is stupid enough to pay a ridiculous amount of money for something that takes no skill at all and only a few minutes—*he* was using *them*. He told himself.

20

That's weird," James mumbled as he sat at Andrew's laptop the next morning. It was Saturday, and his day off, but he was going to mall and stopped by to see if Andrew needed anything. And he wanted to look up something on his laptop.

"What?" Andrew called over from the living room floor, covered with Timmy and Tommy. He enjoyed the boys more these days.

"When you think of famous flute players, you think of Jean-Pierre Rampal, James Galway, and Robert Aitken, but all the flute teachers are women. At least in this area."

When Andrew thought of famous flute players, he came up empty. But he didn't doubt what James had discovered. And he didn't think—*now*, he didn't think that it was because 'Those who can, do, and those who can't, teach.'

"You were thinking of taking flute lessons?"

"Yeah," he smiled shyly. "If I can afford them. Plus, I don't know how much the flute will cost."

James was keying another search. "Same goes for the violin. Menuhin, Perlman, Zukerman, Joshua Bell ... But again all the teachers are women. Were women."

Maybe he could teach himself, he thought, closing the laptop, then heading out.

As soon as he entered the mall, he knew it was a mistake. Whenever he saw two or more young men—boys, really—gathered together, James broke into a sweat. For good reason. Now more than ever because whereas before, their target was often a similar group of girls, now it was almost always lone boys.

Okay, so he'd be quick. He'd get a new notebook and a new knapsack, both at Walmart, then get out.

Walking quickly, he noticed that the mall had become overrun not only by wandering herds of teenaged boys, but also by the homeless. Usually the nooks and crannies were kept empty by Security. Not anymore.

"Hey, you got a couple dollars to spare?" a scruffy-clothed man wobbled up to him.

"No, sorry," James replied. At one time, he would have given the man a couple dollars. And now, he certainly had it. He smiled to himself. He liked his life. He liked Andrew and the boys. He had a job he enjoyed, a job that paid well … But pulling out his wallet would no doubt attract the predatory attention of one of the herds …

He hurried on, but then had to make a pit stop, and saw that another man had set up camp in the cul-de-sac past the restroom.

"What are you looking at?" he challenged.

"Nothing," James said and ducked inside.

A few moments later, as he continued on his way, he wondered about the first man's wobble. Had there been an increase in substance abuse? He grinned a bit at the scholarly tone of his question. He wouldn't be surprised if that was true. His dad was certainly hitting the bottle a lot more than he used to.

Actually, none of the men he saw huddled here and there along the way looked very good. Not taking the situation too well, James thought. And then it suddenly dawned on him. There wouldn't be any more social workers or counsellors to help them out.

But why wasn't Security keeping them out of the mall anymore? It couldn't be because there was less Security, he thought, because that was a male-dominated profession. Though come to think of it, he looked around, he didn't see any uniformed guards. Which was weird. He walked a little more quickly.

Maybe there were too many now? Too many to keep out? And that would be because ... because why? You became homeless when you lost your job. He wasn't sure why men would be losing their jobs, unless they had kids and no one else to look after them, and none of the men he saw so far had any kids with them, but maybe the kids were elsewhere, just running around the mall ...

He'd thought that the women being gone would leave a lot of vacancies. So wouldn't companies want to make it possible for even the men with kids to fill those vacancies? Maybe, he thought, but it took a certain kind of man, a certain kind of person, he corrected, someone without anything to prove, to apply for a job as a bank teller or a cashier ... His dad would rather drink himself to death.

James wished he would, actually. Every evening when he went home, he had to listen to him, "How's my little nanny boy tonight? You want I should get you a little skirt?" And then he'd laugh.

Maybe he should ask Andrew now if he could live in.

Or maybe Security was just too busy elsewhere, he turned his attention back to the here and now, suddenly noticing a herd heading his way. He went into the nearest store.

Fortuitously, it was a computer store.

"Hi, can I help you?" a young man approached him.

"How much does a laptop cost?" James asked. Maybe he could afford that too. Andrew didn't seem to mind that he used his, but it would be nice to have his own.

"Depends on what you want, exactly."

"Just something basic. You know, for going online."

"Okay ... we don't have as many new laptops in stock as we normally do ... How about a refurbished one?" The man showed him several, all of which cost more than he had with him, but not ridiculously more. He thought about calling Andrew and asking if he'd be willing to put it on his credit card over the phone. He'd pay him back—no, actually, Andrew still owed him a bit— But then he thought that if he walked out of the store with a laptop, chances were good he wouldn't make it home with it. Okay, so maybe he could ask Andrew to buy him a laptop in lieu of next week's wages or something.

"Do you accept credit cards over the phone?" James asked.

"We do."

"And do you deliver?" That would make it easier for Andrew.

"We can. It's fifty bucks extra though."

James looked again at the laptops, then wrote down the information about the one that was his first choice. He always had a pen and a small pad of paper with him. In addition to his notebook, which he still had to replace, he reminded himself.

"If I bought this one," James pointed, "does a mouse come with it?"

"No, that would be extra," the man led him into another aisle. "Wireless or corded?"

"Wireless."

"I'd recommend this one," the man pointed, "but this one would do."

James nodded, added the information, then put both pen and notebook back into his pocket.

"Thanks."

"No problem," the man smiled.

James left the store then, looking both ways before he did so.

He passed a lot of stores that were closed, clothing stores mostly, which made sense. No clerks *and* no customers. And, he glanced inside as he passed them, no merchandise. That was a little weird. Wasn't it?

He hoped Walmart was still open.

It was. He quickly went to the school supplies section and picked out a spiral notebook to replace the one— As an afterthought, he took all that was left. Six. He could afford it, and he didn't want to come back any time soon.

Good thing. Because the next time he went to the mall, those notebooks would cost twice as much. It would be like that for a lot of things. Men would refuse to fill women's positions for their pay.

So why had the women not refused? Because if they had demanded more, they wouldn't have gotten the job. Women weren't allowed to negotiate. That's uppity. It presumes you have power.

Also, if they hadn't taken the job, some other woman would've. Some other woman who had a husband paying her way, most of her way, part of her way. Because he was making a 'breadwinner' salary. Or at least what he deserved.

Or some other woman who thought 60% of what she deserved was better than nothing.

James looked in vain for a knapsack. He checked School Supplies, then Sports, then Luggage. No knapsacks. In fact, no a lot of stuff. He couldn't make any sense of it. Why were some shelves full and others empty? Maybe Walmart didn't get all their stuff from the same place? And some places—no, that didn't make sense. The women were gone all over, weren't they?

He tried to remember if any of the stores he'd passed that were open might carry knapsacks.

And because he was trying to remember, he forgot to look both ways when he exited the store. By the time he realized that one of the herds was near, and heading straight for him, he was too far away to make it back inside. He looked around in panic, then made a run for the custodian near the bench and trash bin. He was a big guy who looked more like a security guard than a custodian.

"Oh look, he's hiding!" the lead beast sang out, as James cowered behind the large man.

But the custodian just stared them down, mop in hand like a weapon.

"Come out, come out, wherever you are!" the young man, boy, taunted. The others snickered. James stayed put.

The custodian continued to stare them down.

After a minute of no action, they got bored and wandered off.

"Thanks," James said, when it was safe to come out from behind the man.

"No problem," the man said. "I saw you coming. And they make my life hell upending all the bins in the food court. Walking evidence of the need for free contraception and abortion on demand, every one of them!"

James grinned.

"You, on the other hand," the man sighed. "Best not come back to the mall. They've taken it over."

James nodded. Just like they'd taken over the high school.

Why do we let them rule the world, he wondered.

Okay, next stop, the music store. Before he'd left Andrew's place, James had written down the addresses of two stores that sold musical instruments. And he'd brought his public transit map, so he could take the subway and then the bus.

Or just the bus. Taking the subway took forever because every time a small herd got on, he had to get off and either slip into another car or wait for the next train. At least with the bus, he could sit as close as possible to the driver. Who, unknown to him, had pepper spray in his pocket. Wouldn't stop a bullet, but it might make a knife miss its mark. What else could he do?

An hour later, James disembarked just a block from the first music store. On the way, he passed a second-hand store that might, he thought, have a knapsack. It had two in fact. One was turquoise, and truthfully he kind of liked that one because it made him think of the Caribbean seas or something, but he knew the colour would attract the herds, go figure, so he chose the brown one. It was a good size, had lots of pockets, which he liked, and was in excellent shape except for what looked like a small coffee stain on the back. It had a name tag inside—Brendan Fowler? Forler? He couldn't tell. No matter. He paid the ten dollars and carried on.

A bell over the door of the music store jingled as he opened it, and a grey-haired man came out from the back room.

"Hello," he said, pleasantly.

"Hello," James said. "Do you sell flutes? And do you know of anyone who teaches the flute?"

"You'd like to learn to play the flute, would you?" the man seemed delighted.

"I would."

"Excellent. Not many young men choose the flute, they're all busy with their electric guitars and their drums ... but the flute is a fine instrument, a subtle instrument," he led James to a display. "We have a fine selection, but I suspect you don't quite know what you want yet, is that right?"

"Yes. I mean, I'm a beginner, so I guess I want a beginner flute."

The man smiled. "Well said. And you won't want to spend a lot of money in case it doesn't work out. Though," he looked hard at James, "I suspect you have the discipline and the desire. That's really all you need." He reached into the display case and made a selection. This is a second-hand flute, but there is absolutely nothing wrong with it. It has a very nice tone," the man played a few phrases from a sad song, then played a bit of a jig. James smiled.

"It's only $99.99, and it comes with the case."

"Really? That's good!" He'd expected to pay twice that. "And what about books?"

"Normally your teacher would tell you which books to buy ... You asked when you came in if I knew any teachers, and I'm afraid I don't. Or rather I do, but— They're all gone." He still couldn't quite believe it. "It's a tragedy, what's happened."

James nodded.

"However," the man rallied, "let's see if we can find you a good teach-yourself book, shall we?"

"Yes, please. That would be great."

The man led James to the flute section of the books, and they spent some time looking through the books until they found one that James thought he could learn from on his own, from scratch. They decided that since the books were intended for students a bit younger than James, it would not be a waste of money for him to go ahead and purchase the first three in the series.

The man opened the case and added a cleaning rod and cloth, explaining to James how to take care of his new flute. James paid, and then carefully put everything into the knapsack along with the half dozen spiral notebooks.

"Thank you," he said as he left.

"Thank *you*," the man said, smiling. "I look forward to seeing you when you come back for Book Four. Bring your flute and play something for me!"

"I will!"

21

As for what had been on all those empty shelves, it had been made in sweatshops—by, primarily, women. *Women* had been turning materials into the goods that filled over 80% of the store's shelves. Any store's shelves. Every store's shelves.

Which is why eventually—initially they just assumed the women would have their little fun then come back—Bill Rutherford, CEO of Stride Enterprises, and Henry Billings, CFO of Stride Enterprises, had a golf meeting. Tried to have a golf meeting. Martha had always taken care of the arrangements. In coordination with Doreen. Now, first one of the men had to call the other. Bill didn't know Henry's extension offhand. And he didn't know where to look for it. Finally, on the Monday of that second week, when the women still hadn't returned, he just went on over to Henry's office. But Henry wasn't there. And of course he couldn't just leave a message with Doreen. Doreen wasn't there either. Bill patted his pockets for pen and paper, to leave a message under his door, but nothing. So he had to walk all the way back to his own office, write out a message, then walk all the way back and slip it under Henry's door. Appalling, really.

When Henry found the message, he tried to call Bill.

"Doreen, put me through to Bill," he said when he picked up the receiver. And promptly felt like a fool. Like Bill, he didn't have a directory. Why would he? Like Bill, he eventually just walked over to his office. Fortunately, Bill was there.

Then there was the sorting out of their calendars. Again, Martha and Doreen had taken care of all that. They didn't know where they were supposed to be when. Both had missed several important meetings on that first Friday, the following Saturday, and then every day of the following week. They suspected as much, but weren't exactly sure what they'd missed, since, when the parties who'd been stood up tried to call, they were fed into the company's Muzak holding pattern for longer than they were willing to wait. Which was about forty-five seconds.

"Enough of this!" Bill said. He walked to his door, stuck his head out, and called down the hall. "Aaron!"

Aaron, COO, sighed, got up out of his chair, and headed to Bill's office. "Yes?" he said. Coldly.

"Set up a tee time for Henry and me."

The man's eyes bulged. "I beg your pardon?"

"We need to talk. And we want to do it over a game of golf. Make it happen."

Aaron left Bill's office. And would have left the building, then and there, for good, except that he thought of an alternative.

"Richard!"

A week later they finally had their meeting. Sixteen days after the women had disappeared. They showed up at the golf course, each in their expensive car. It was Sunday. It was two o'clock.

"I'm sorry, sir, but we have no reservation for you for two o'clock."

"Of course you do!" Bill insisted. "It was arranged a week ago. Are you telling me we can't tee off?"

"I'm afraid that's exactly what I'm telling you, sir."

"Look here, I've been a member of this club for longer than you've been alive! Where's the manager?" he bellowed. Henry cringed a little.

An older man came running.

"What seems to be the problem?"

"This ... *boy* mucked up the reservations and now he's saying we can't tee off!"

The man checked the reservation book handed to him by the young man standing anxiously at his shoulder.

"I'm afraid, yes, there has been some mix-up in the reservations. We do apologize. Would you like to retire to the Oak Room while you wait? Anything you'd care to order, compliments of the house. I'll let them know."

"Oh for Christ's sake," Bill fumed.

"Let's just go have a drink," Henry suggested.

So they went to the club's bar, choosing a quiet table in the corner. Bill flicked his hand in the air to indicate that he wanted something, attention certainly, but no one came running.

After ten minutes, they got up, walked over to the bar, asked the bartender for what they wanted, then returned to their table. Terribly appalling.

"So we have a problem here," Henry started, though he was using the word to mean something considerably different from what was meant by those who had been lobbying for years to get the company to clean up its act in its overseas sweatshops.

"Yes, the boys in Marketing are giving me grief. They say they can't sell anything without sex!" Bill laughed.

Oh, that's interesting, Henry thought. He hadn't actually thought of that. As it turned out, Marketing quickly realized that they didn't need to use real women. In fact, they hadn't used real women for ages. Not since image editing software was developed. Men could be, were, easily influenced by exaggerations, distortions—lies. In fact, the less real, the better.

Truthfully, Henry suspected that Marketing's budget was overly inflated. In fact, the entire Marketing department was superfluous. *Should be* superfluous. If someone needs or wants something, they'll buy it. Without advertising. And if they don't need or want it, we shouldn't be making it, he thought. Then sighed. Linda had been right. It was time he retired. God how he missed her! But he couldn't retire. Not now. What would he do in an empty house all day? They'd had plans for his retirement, they were going to *do* things, *go* places. And now she— They say you're not supposed to make major decisions when you're grieving. Okay, so he wouldn't retire just yet.

"Marketing's the least of our worries, Bill," he said.

"What's that?" Bill cupped his hand to his ear.

Speaking about time to retire …

"We've lost 90% of our labour force in manufacturing. Our factories overseas—" Henry had a quick thought. The Olympics would have to be cancelled because no one would have running shoes. He giggled a little. Which made him realize—definitely time to retire.

"This thing with the women? Is that what you're referring to?"

"It doesn't matter that Marketing can't advertise, because in a week, there won't be anything to advertise. The factories will be empty."

"So we hire replacements. We've done it before. Whenever they get all upset about something or other and go on strike, you remember—"

"I doubt the men will work for fifty cents an hour. I've told you before, Bill, we need to clean up our act. We can't keep sweeping our messes under the carpet."

In some countries, Henry knew, it was the women who hauled water. What was happening there, he wondered. Would the men be annoyed to have to take time out from killing each other to get their own water? Or would they make the smallest and the weakest their new bitches? As the lads would say.

"What are you talking about?" Bill almost shouted. "Every time some bleeding heart goes on about the working conditions, we send someone over there, and it's all good."

How can he be so naïve? Henry wondered. Well, he can't be. He's just been bullshitting so long he believes his own bullshit.

"That's because they know we're coming. We need to put our own men there. Permanently. Make sure the women—the workers—can go to the bathroom when they need to for god's sake." That had been one of the complaints that had struck him the most. Women had developed bladder infections from trying to hold it.

"And we should be paying them a helluva lot more than twenty cents an hour," Henry added.

"We do that, we'll lose investors, you know that."

Henry sighed. He did know that. They were between a rock and a hard place. If they made all the changes they should, they wouldn't be able to compete with those who didn't, and they'd go bankrupt. It was an old story. An old failure. Asking consumers to buy fair trade, so to speak, didn't work, because consumers were just as bad as upper management and investors: they put personal gain before justice.

So what was the solution? Government mandated fair pay and fair prices? Of course, that had already happened to some extent— there were laws stipulating minimum wage. So what was stopping us from doing more, Henry wondered. What was stopping the government from mandating more?

The people who made their shoes got paid fifty cents an hour, but then the retailers turned around and sold them for over a hundred bucks. That wasn't fair. The people who made the stuff should get at least half of what the stuff sold for. He'd read recently that a two dollar meal of a burger and fries actually cost forty cents. Where did the rest go? Advertising. Transport. Administration. All the people who handled the product. All of whom got paid a hundred, *four* hundred, times more than the ones who made the product. How had that come to be? How is it the guy who drove the truck that moved the shoes from point A to point B got paid four hundred times more than the woman who actually *made* the shoes?

But if they did it right, everything would cost, well, *so* much more than it did.

Maybe that would be a good thing, Henry thought. Maybe then people would buy only what they really needed, only what they really wanted. Maybe then we wouldn't have turned into a nation of *consumers*. The very word turned his stomach. Definitely time to retire.

"Besides," Bill said, "fifty cents an hour to them is a lot of money. They're better off working for us than working the streets. And they know it."

Marginally better, Henry thought. And even so, that was no reason not to pay them what their work was worth.

In the end, they did send their own people over to manage the companies. They decided to increase the pay for the remaining boys, reduce the working day from 12 hours to 8 hours, let them sit down while they worked, let them go to the bathroom if they needed to … the list was long. As a result, many young men who would have otherwise joined the army—joined *an* army—applied for a job at their company instead. But it wasn't enough.

And it took a while. A long while. Once decisions had been made as to who to station at their overseas companies, it was weeks before flights could be booked. And months before those flights actually occurred. Because they couldn't just ask Ellen in HR to take care of it. Ellen in HR was gone. So was, essentially,

Reservations. At every airline. And because 90% of the flight attendants had been female, 90% of the flights had been cancelled.

Yes, certainly, replacements were being trained. Everywhere. But that would also take a while. A long while. Because what women had been doing wasn't as easy as they'd been making it look. (And why was that? Henry wondered. Why *did* women make things look so easy, with a ready smile and a cheerful disposition …) In the case of airline attendants, for example, replacement trainees had to learn aviation regulations, airport codes, aircraft configurations, airline terminology, national and international geography, first aid, and, often, another language. And most men refused to do all that for a starting salary of $25,000. Not when they used to make twice that. To do whatever it was they'd been doing instead.

And of course, it wasn't just knapsacks that were made in sweatshops. Electronics were also made in sweatshops. By women. So when James asked Andrew to buy him that laptop in lieu of the following week's wages, it was too late. The store he'd visited, and most others like it, had closed. Their shelves were empty. There would be no more laptops, or tablets, or phones, or mp3 players …

Or NFL jerseys. They were also made in sweatshops. By women. And any jerseys already made were just sitting in a warehouse somewhere. Because the clerical force that had arranged golf meetings and hotel accommodations had also arranged international communications, trade shipments, money transfers …

Bottom line, none of the teams would get new jerseys that year. And that's when the situation really made the news.

22

Even as they said how many businesses had gone bankrupt that day, even as they said that a stock market crash was imminent, they didn't admit that it was due to the women's absence. The world was fast approaching total economic collapse, and yet …

Marcus was watching the news. He'd gone to Brendan's funeral that Sunday afternoon and couldn't summon the energy to do anything productive that evening. He took another swallow from his rum and soda and switched channels. You'd never have known it.

It was the global warming thing all over again, he thought. It's right in front of us, we're on a high-speed collision course with environmental disaster, and yet the only thing mainstream media give us is the weather report. Not the climate report. Oh sure, they've upped the drama of the weather reports—they've added exciting visuals and the weatherperson uses commanding gestures to suggest exacting detail—but it's all a sham. There's no *real* information being provided. No mention of how close we are to the point of no return, no mention of what, exactly—and we do know—that would mean. And it's as if global warming just … happened. No one was responsible. For the droughts, the hurricanes, the floods …

Of course that's because the people who *are* responsible, the oil magnates, for starters, forbid the media to say so. That's why they've *bought* the media, in one way or another.

But there's no need for a cover up in this case, so—ah. To attribute the economic collapse to the disappearance of women would be to acknowledge their role, their work, their value—their power.

Every business, hell almost every endeavour, was built like a house of cards. Men were so obsessed with power, hierarchy was a given; they couldn't even *imagine* organizing any other way. They were at the top (of course) and in the middle (trying to climb to the top), but at the base, there was a phalanx of women. Take that away and the house of cards flutters to the ground. It may take an hour, a day, a week, a year. But all fall down, they will.

If a CEO has ten women to do his bidding, when they're gone, he'll become one-tenth as productive. If a man has only one woman to do his bidding, his wife, he'll become half as productive. Simple math.

Of course, CEOs don't have a team of ten women, but the way business is set up, it amounts to that. And most wives don't do their husband's bidding, but Marcus was sure they did a lot of 'invisible work' as Beth once put it.

So. Productivity decreased, clients were lost, revenue decreased; supplies decreased, customers were lost, revenue decreased; profits plummeted, layoffs occurred; productivity and supplies decreased even more; revenue decreased even more; profits plummeted even further; investors disappeared; companies went under. And when men lost their assistants, their jobs—not to mention their cheerleaders, their sexual outlets, and their punching bags— When men lost, they got angry. And they expressed their anger with violence. It was a perfect storm.

The bars and the beer and liquor stores were booming.

Marcus raised his glass to the screen.

He wondered what was happening in other countries. In countries where women weren't allowed to work. If their schools, hospitals, businesses were already run completely by men ... The irony.

23

Andrew supposed he was lucky he still had a job, but when the paycheques finally got processed and deposited, he was in for a rude shock. His take-home pay for the past month was half of what it had been. HALF!

He stormed toward Richard's office immediately. Then stopped just outside the door to calm himself. No doubt it was just a mistake. No doubt someone was trying to take care of Payroll just like he was trying to take care of Reception.

"There must have been some mistake," he said, trying to keep the strain out of his voice. "My paycheque—who do I see in Payroll?"

Richard held out his hand to take the statement Andrew had been holding, then took a look.

"Oh no, my boy," he chuckled. Making light of Andrew's concerns. "Surely you don't think that answering the phones should be paid as much as project management?"

Actually, he hadn't. Until now. Now he realized that answering the phones was as difficult—*more* difficult—than project management. It was stressful, handling five lines at a time, *and* dealing with walk-ins, *and* doing everyone's photocopying. He had less autonomy, less freedom. For hours at a stretch, he couldn't even get up and leave the desk. He certainly couldn't just walk around for a bit when he felt like it. He realized, just then, that he was defining 'difficult' in a new, broader, way.

"There's no supervisory responsibility attached to the position," Richard continued. "As project manager, you oversaw the work of other people."

That was true.

"Pay scale accords with supervisory responsibility," Richard said, gesturing out the door, implying that he deserved his huge salary because he oversaw the entire floor.

Andrew had accepted that as the reason, one of the reasons, for his higher pay. He supervised Sharon, for example; therefore, he made more than Sharon.

But now he wondered whether there wasn't something wrong with the way they figured out salaries, with the weights they assigned to various factors. After all, Sharon didn't need his supervision. She was quite capable of doing her job without him. He suspected that was true of most people. More often than not, supervisors got in the way of doing your job, he thought.

"I'm responsible for what you do," Richard went on, seeing the uncertainty on Andrew's face. "If you mess up, I get called to task for it."

Actually, you don't, Andrew thought. If I mess up, *I'm* the one who'll get called to task. I'm the one who'll get fired. Not you.

The phone rang. Richard raised his eyebrows and ever so slightly nodded Andrew back to Reception.

Andrew hesitated, then wisely decided not to push it. He went back to his desk. His new desk.

"Stride Enterprises," he answered the call, then transferred it to Simon.

He looked again at the statement Richard had returned to him. Minus what he'd been paying James, he'd been working for ... $2.00/hour. Two dollars an hour. He couldn't live on that. He couldn't even pay rent on that.

He'd have to reduce James' wages. It wasn't fair. It wasn't right. But.

Matthew came out of his office, plopped a thick report onto the table beside the printer/copier, and said cheerily, "Ten copies, collated, by noon."

Andrew gave his back the finger. The phone rang.

Of course he considered quitting.

He hated the job. It was simultaneously more difficult and less challenging than being a Project Manager.

And it was humiliating. He didn't go to university for four years to answer the phone or stand at a photocopier for hours on end. All of his former colleagues, except Kyle, who had disappeared at the end of that first week, acted like his bosses now, ordering him around, treating him like their subordinate. They couldn't see past the position, the role, to the person. He was now the receptionist; therefore, he was now their inferior. He wanted to shout 'Hey I'm still Andrew, I'm still a Project Manager, I still have the same skills, qualifications, status, and authority as I did before!' But of course he didn't. Not the last two.

They'd even started telling him to clean up the place a bit. Coffee that was spilled on the lunchroom counter stayed spilled. All day. The lunch table became sticky and covered in crumbs. Custodial still came every night, he saw the guy a couple times when he was late leaving, but Sharon or Brianna (he finally figured out that that was her name) must have given everything a swipe now and then during the day. Cleaning up after them. My god, but they were all a bunch of children.

Bottom line, he'd never worked so hard at a job in his life.

And still, it wasn't good enough. Richard had come to him one day, to say that new clients were down. Way down.

"What the hell are you saying to people when they call to inquire?" he demanded.

"Nothing."

And maybe that was the problem. There was no smile in his voice when he answered the phone, no suggestion that it would be nice to bring their business to Stride.

Quite apart from all the calls he simply didn't get to. He didn't tell Richard about those. But he couldn't answer three calls at once. By the time he'd finished with one call, the other two had hung up. It wasn't his fault they were too impatient to hold.

"I don't understand the problem, Andrew. All you have to do is answer the goddamn phone! That's a simple enough thing, isn't it?"

The day he'd finally fixed the printer, he'd taken the phone off the hook for the duration. He'd found the manual, discovered that the toner needed to be replaced, found a box of new toner in the cupboard under the printer, then figured out how to replace the old one with a new one. It had taken only twenty minutes. So much for men's technological proficiency, nay, superiority. He had also been taking the phone off the hook when he did the photocopying.

In fact, this whole past month—had it been only a month?—he'd never worked so hard, period. Answering five phones all day, doing everyone's photocopying, and running errands for everyone on the floor—do this, do that—he had to do three things and be in two places at once all day from the minute he arrived to the minute he went home.

And then at home, from the minute he arrived, Timmy and Tommy demanded his attention. James was good, but he wasn't Daddy. They'd whine, they'd cry, they'd shriek— "Daddy, come here!" "Daddy, look!" Daddy, do this, Daddy, do that—

It would get better, he told himself. It would get easier as they got older. Wait a minute—was he imagining the rest of his life without Diane? Well, truthfully, he'd imagined that even before this had happened. But he'd imagined she'd take the kids with her. He'd just see them on the weekends. It would be fun. Not work.

Not that being with the kids was work— At least, not as he'd defined it, up to now— But at the end of the day, he was just so … drained. The kids were always there, always needing something.

He'd had not one weekend, not one whole evening, barely even one whole hour to himself. Except at night when the kids had gone to bed. And then he was too damn tired to do anything.

There had been no more squash games at lunch, no more after-work drinks with the guys, no more golf games on the weekend …

There had to be a better way.

So late one night, when he finally had some time to himself, he looked at the classifieds. But all the ads were for receptionists, secretaries, teachers, cashiers, tellers … If he stayed at Stride, then at least when, if, the women came back, he'd get his old job back. Right?

And then James went missing.

He was fine, he was there, that Friday when Andrew went home. He'd heard him as he'd come out of the stairwell, practising his flute, playing the Batman theme for the boys. They'd had dinner, and then James had left.

But then his father, Arnie, pounded on Andrew's door the next morning.

Andrew peeked through the peephole, saw who it was, and opened the door.

"What the fuck are you doing with my son? Jimmy?" He pushed his way into Andrew's apartment. "Jimmy?" he called out again and looked around.

Timmy and Tommy started crying. Andrew rushed to stand in front of them. "James isn't here. He goes home at six-thirty. You know that," Andrew replied, confused. That was the routine. James showed up at eight, half an hour before Andrew had to leave, stayed with the kids all day, did whatever house stuff needed to be done, then when Andrew got home at five-thirty, they all ate the dinner James had prepared—'all' including, now, Mr. Begonia—and then as soon as he'd cleaned up the kitchen, he went home, to his dad's apartment.

"You mean he's not here?" Arnie processed Andrew's words quickly, all things considered.

"No," Andrew was right behind him. "You mean he's not at home?"

"No," he reached up and scratched his crew cut. "I figured he'd stayed here overnight. I—"

They both immediately thought the worst. Well, no, actually, they didn't. They both immediately thought he'd been beaten up again.

Arnie went back to his apartment to get the keys to his truck.

Andrew went for his phone to call the police and report him missing. The line was busy.

He bundled the boys into his car as quickly as he could and started cruising the neighbourhood, looking for James huddled in some alleyway.

Arnie was doing the same thing, sweeping further and further from the apartment.

24

A ndrew searched all morning, unsuccessfully, then went back to his apartment. He made lunch for the kids—they'd been *so* good in the car all morning— Well, no, that wasn't quite true. They'd been despondent. Losing James was sort of like losing Diane all over again. That they'd been so quiet was, in truth, a little disturbing.

After lunch, he went out again to search a bit more. He correctly anticipated that the boys would fall asleep in the car. Andrew considered stopping at a police station to make a report, but that last time he went to a station … Besides, James hadn't yet been missing for twenty-four hours, so they probably wouldn't even take his report. And he'd probably have to wait in line for an hour to be told that.

A short while later, he finally accepted that driving around simply hoping to see him was a waste of time. He'd already covered every street, every alley, every parking lot—everywhere he might see him huddled, too hurt to move. Nothing.

Besides, the boys had woken up. Timmy had started crying, Tommy was whining, understandably … He returned to the apartment.

After settling the kids in front of the TV with a snack and one of their favourite movies—Tommy half-heartedly chose one from their DVD box—Andrew went online to see if there was anything on the 'up-to-the-minute' news channels. Maybe, just maybe, there would be a report that someone had found him …

No such luck.

When he checked on the boys, he saw that they had fallen asleep again, so he gently relocated them to their bedroom, got himself a beer, then turned on the TV. He idly surfed for a while then stopped to listen to something about the childcare situation.

"But Kevin, the thing we have to ask," one commentator was saying to the other in one of those fake, scripted debates, "is whose responsibility are they? Should the government be providing free daycare? Or should that be a benefit provided by employers to their employees?"

"Or should children be the sole responsibility of the parents?" Kevin smiled charmingly into the camera. "After all, Ashton, it's not like the stork makes deliveries willy nilly."

"Indeed," Ashton laughed good-naturedly.

Andrew grimaced. The debate was a little overdue.

He didn't realize what an understatement that was.

"Some men are taking matters into their own hands," Ashton continued—so much for the debate, Andrew thought, as there had been no arguments made for either view— "and have re-opened the daycares that have closed. But others point out that the men aren't qualified daycare teachers. Still others say that men don't have the disposition to deal with—and I quote one of our viewers who sent in this comment—'ten or twenty squalling infants all day'," he grinned into the camera.

You got that right, Andrew thought. He wouldn't leave either of his kids with most of the men he knew. They'd be thrown against the wall within an hour.

But did *women* have the 'disposition' to deal with squalling infants? Seriously, that can't be chromosome-linked. So, what, did women just try harder to be patient? Maybe they were climbing the walls just as much. He wondered how often a mother lost it and threw her kid against the wall.

"And I imagine," Kevin offered, "that many parents would be concerned about leaving their small children with *men*." He didn't spell it out. But it was there, hanging in the air. Simply put, men didn't trust other men not to hurt their kids.

Which says a lot, Andrew thought. He'd been starting to feel not very proud to be a man. Since.

"Yes," Ashton responded, "I understand that the daycares and schools that *are* running—"

"Schools too?" Kevin asked, though of course he already knew the answer.

"Yes, there have been attempts to re-open some of the elementary schools …"

Bet they found that not as easy as they thought, Andrew said to himself. 'Those who can, do; those who can't, teach' my ass. They'd know *nothing* about child psychology, child development— He'd been reading the book James had brought home from the library. It was an eye-opener. Something like that should be mandatory, he'd said to himself part way through, for everyone who wanted to deal with kids. In a professional capacity *and* in a personal capacity.

"… and to alleviate parents' concerns, what they've had to do is install video surveillance cameras in all the classrooms."

Not very proud at all.

Andrew turned off the TV and fretted a bit more about James.

But he also worried about Monday. He couldn't take the kids to work with him again. If he did, he'd be fired. And he couldn't lose his job, poorly paid though it was. More so because it *was* so poorly paid. In a couple months, he'd have *nothing* in reserve.

He thought about the quasi-debate. He had to admit that he couldn't justify expecting his employer to bear the burden of his kids. Or other people, through their taxes. Having kids was his choice, a consequence of his actions. *He* was responsible for them.

It's just— It was impossible to meet that responsibility. The way society was set up, he simply couldn't. Not by himself. Ah. Hence the nuclear family.

Well, no, he thought, not necessarily. He and James had a pretty workable arrangement. Having—nurturing—kids just required a partnership. Not necessarily a marriage. Aha! He should join forces with Kyle or Simon or someone. Like in that old TV show … *Kate and Allie*. The 'partner' need not be the mother of his kids.

He called Kyle. He hadn't known him well, couldn't actually remember why he had his number, but …

"Hey, Kyle, it's Andrew. From Stride," he thought to add. "How are you?"

"Not so good, man, how 'bout you?"

"Oh well, you know … Listen, I was thinking—I'm in a bit of a jam with this whole childcare and work thing … The kid I'd hired as a sort of nanny has gone missing, and it occurred to me that the smart thing to do would be to just get a roommate, sort of, a—"

"Yes."

"Yes? Just like that?"

"Got a fucking eviction notice today. Got laid off that first week, as you know …"

Actually, Andrew hadn't known. He had, at some point, noticed that Kyle wasn't around anymore, but he'd thought maybe he was just using his sick days and holidays …

"So … you've got a kid, right?"

"Yeah. Evan. He's eight. And you?"

"Timmy, two, and Tommy, four."

"That's rough."

"Tell me about it."

"So what exactly did you have in mind?"

"Well, I'm just sort of thinking out loud here," Andrew said, "but while I'm at Stride all day, you could be here all day doing the kid care and the house stuff, and I'd pay you—"

"Half."

"Half?" Andrew hesitated.

"By 'house stuff,' you mean everything, right? Meals, clean up after, dusting, vacuuming, bathroom—"

"Dusting?"

"Yeah, you don't dust?"

"I—"

"And doesn't Timmy crawl around on the floor? So I'd have to keep that clean too."

James had done more than he'd realized. So had Diane, he thought belatedly.

"Bottom line, we'll both be working all day, do we really want to debate whose job is more important or more difficult?"

"No, I guess not. But," Andrew did the math, "that means each of us will be making just $11 an hour. We'd go fifty-fifty on rent, electricity, and food, right?"

"Wait a minute, how do you figure $11?"

"I'm not making Project Manager salary anymore. Richard's paying me what Brianna made."

"You're kidding." Kyle processed that. "Jesus."

"Yeah." Andrew took another swallow his beer. Might be the last for a while.

"What's your rent? Etc."

Andrew told him.

"So, what, do we bring in a third partner?" Andrew had just thought of that. No need for everything to be in twos.

"Or I can try to get a job evenings. While *you* do the kid care and the house stuff."

"And we'd split *your* salary fifty-fifty as well?"

"Yeah. No wait," Kyle said, "if I do all the house stuff during the day, there won't be any house stuff that you need to do. So we split my salary, I don't know, sixty-forty? Seventy-thirty?"

"Or you leave half the house stuff for me to do."

"You don't want to come home after a day at Stride and do house stuff."

"No, but you won't want to do eight hours kid care *and* house stuff and then go in for an eight-hour shift of something."

"True enough."

"Maybe we can just agree to work out the fine points if and when."

"Okay. By then I'll have some idea maybe of what's fair if we split the house stuff."

"Deal." Andrew wondered then why he and Diane hadn't had this conversation. They just seemed to assume that she would do all the kid and house stuff during the day and he'd just come home and do … nothing. Or next to.

"One caveat."

Andrew waited.

"If you have explosive diarrhea or something, *you* clean it up. I'll keep the bathroom clean in a general way, but extenuating circumstances? I'm not cleaning up your shit."

"Agreed."

Andrew realized then that Diane had been doing just that. Must be hard to see your husband as some kind of sexy when you're cleaning up his shit.

25

Darryl had been having a fucked up week. Couple weeks. His car's fender was still bashed in, the insurance company still hadn't paid, his lawyer was a total dick, his MP was useless, and his neighbourhood was becoming overrun with bums and druggies.

"Get a fucking job!" he'd screamed at them just the night before. He would've told them to get the fuck into rehab or the shelter, but why should *he* pay for their problems?

He swore to himself that if they were there again when he went home tonight, he'd break their fucking kneecaps.

In the meantime, he was taking a well-deserved break from the list of installs he was supposed to be making.

"Darryl?"

Shit. His supervisor. The one and only Dickhead Dick.

"Yeah?" he hit the company screensaver, then looked up from his computer.

"Aren't you supposed to be—never mind," the man shook his head. "I've got another job for you. I'm going to put Scott on installs. Come with me."

Come with me. What, not even a 'Please'? Yes sir, right away sir, fuck you sir.

Darryl followed the man down the hall, down the stairs, down into—the basement?

He unlocked a door and stepped through into a large room. Darryl followed.

"As you know, we've been storing our out-of-commission units here, intending to donate them or recycle them ... whenever whoever made up their minds ... But we're going to bring them back into service. It's getting harder and harder to get new units, as you know, and for many tasks, these will do just fine. So, if you could make a start today ..."

Darryl stood there in disbelief. Didn't even notice that Dickhead Dick had left. There were rows and rows of shelves containing grimy gray keyboards, clunky LCD monitors, desktops and towers, probably 486s, maybe even some 386s ... And he was supposed to work on this ... *garbage?*

A man can take only so much. Darryl walked out to his car, opened his trunk, got out the baseball bat he'd acquired after that incident on the road, returned to the basement storage room, and smashed all of the monitors, and then the computers.

Every last one of them.

26

James had gone out for an evening walk. He was working on a new poem, wrestling with 'tumbling like …'. 'Tumbling like tom toms'? He liked how it sounded, all tumbly, but it didn't really make sense. It was the sounds of the tom toms that tumbled, not the tom toms themselves. And actually, even the sounds were more rigidly rhythmic than tumbling …

Even as he thought, he was vigilant, but since he was in a quiet residential area—he stuck to the route he took during the day with Timmy and Tommy—he didn't anticipate any need to run. In fact, when the van pulled up beside him, he slowed, thinking they were going to stop and ask for directions.

They did stop. And as one man rolled down the window, two others got out the back, grabbed him before he knew what was happening, and shoved him inside.

As it pulled away, he hollered and banged on the doors and the sides of the van, but to no avail. He quickly realized that it would be smarter to conserve his strength. And make a run for it as soon as they opened the doors.

About an hour later, he had his chance. He had felt the van stop and was ready. But it was dark, he stumbled, and, in any case, the compound was fenced.

He was taken to a large room, much like a barn, in which there were a dozen other young men. Each had a cot and a blanket. There was a single bathroom in the corner. They were fed once a day.

More than once a day they were put into service.

"Oh, you like this, don't you," the man groaned as he thrust his cock into James' rectum. James screamed with unbearable pain. "Oh, that's good, you little bitch, scream some more, tell me you like it."

Another time they double-teamed him, forcing him onto all fours, one man thrusting from behind, the other thrusting into his mouth. A third masturbated and then squirted his cum all over James' face. It was called a facial. Another urinated on him. That was called a golden shower.

"Don't eat," the boy beside him whispered, when they brought food.

"No talking!" the man shouted.

James later understood. If you don't eat, you won't have to shit.

"Here," the man threw a blond wig at him. "Put that on."

James obeyed. But his hair was growing quickly, and soon he wouldn't need a wig.

The man also threw some lipstick at him. "And fix yourself up a little, you look like a mess."

What? James was incredulous. How was he supposed to look in these circumstances?

"And when we take you out, smile. You got that?"

"Ask for more," the man commanded.

"More," James winced.

"And say please."

"Please."

"Louder, bitch!"

"More, please!" James screamed through his tears.

And then one time—he was so crazed with pain he didn't realize it at first—there was an audience. He heard them urging the man on, "Pound him harder, drill him, give the little cunt what he deserves."

"Oh yeah, that'll teach him!"

Teach me what, James would have wondered, if he could've formed a coherent thought.

The man pulled on James' shoulders, forcing his back to arch.

"Oh yeah, break the bitch!" The men cheered. And laughed.

He hadn't known that 30 million men, 20% of the male population, would pay to do these things to him. In the U.S. alone.

He hadn't known that men would spend $3,000 per second to watch other men do these things to him. That every second, 30,000 men were watching porn.

He hadn't known that almost all porn involved violence, degradation, humiliation. That that was rather the point, as so many johns would say, had said, when interviewed.

He hadn't known that the porn industry made more money than the NFL, the NBA, and major league baseball combined. More than NBC, CBS, and ABC combined. More than Microsoft, Google, Amazon, eBay, Yahoo, and Apple. Combined.

He hadn't known that he would have to 'service' 40 men each day before he'd be given food or allowed sleep. That at $25 each, he'd be making $1,000 a day. For his handlers.

He hadn't known that there were six-year-olds in the compound.

And he hadn't known that they had other plans for him. Pretty little white boy like him? With the pouty lips, the pale complexion, and the curls? He was a regular Little Lord Fauntleroy. They were going to sell him to the sex tourists in Asia. Again and again.

Good thing he was raped to death first.

The phrase 'raped to death' sounds so … innocuous. One should wonder how a phrase that includes both 'raped' and 'death' *can* sound innocuous. And yet, it does. You figure it out.

In any case, it doesn't describe the way his rectum was ripped to shreds. The last man thrust so forcefully, and maybe not with his penis, that he perforated James' bowel. When James died of internal bleeding a few days later, he was no good to them anymore, so they just dumped him.

He was lucky. It had been only a month.

27

It was Justin who stumbled upon him. He'd been weaving his way home, drunk, stoned, what did it matter.

28

Funding for his research hadn't come through yet, but Marcus wasn't surprised. Even when things were normal, the process took six months. The men he'd enlisted agreed to proceed anyway, on a voluntary basis, even though doing something without pay, giving it away, was, for most men, against the grain.

As they worked through the developmental stages, Marcus continued to put thoughts to paper, but none of the op-eds or guest blog posts he'd written, none of the pitches to magazines and radio programs he'd made ... Even before, mainstream media were reluctant to focus on women—unless the story was about kids, cooking, interior decorating, or their physical appearance (their make-up, their hair, their weight, their clothing). Now, they were even more resistant.

On the other hand, with impressive efficiency many academic journals scrapped their in-progress issues and published instead preliminary thoughts, theories, findings ... But no one read academic journals except other academics. And the academic male was low on the totem pole. Unless he worked in math, science, or engineering. Why was that, Marcus had often wondered. Men were fascinated with how things worked, okay, but then why didn't they want to know how they themselves worked? The exception to this rule seemed to be when they could use that knowledge to manipulate others. *Then* psychology and sociology became of value.

As for poetry, music, all of the other arts—frivolous. When did men lose their sense of beauty? When had it become so narrowly defined, perverted, as sexual attractiveness?

He continued to watch mainstream media—indeed, media coverage had become one strand of their proposed research project—and one evening, he saw an item on the news about the emergent 'pretty boy trade.' They actually called it a 'trade', Marcus noted. Which implies voluntary consent, if not some sort of equality of exchange. Which, of course, would be a lie.

But not a new one.

He sighed. Women's subordination had been so systemic, it had been unremarkable. Now that the women had disappeared, and men had to take their places, fill their roles, the subordination was becoming noteworthy. Newsworthy.

He sighed again. He'd concluded, soon after the women had disappeared, that there were two ways it could go. Either they, the men, would finally see the double standards, the sexism, and make corrections. Or they would just create a new subordinate class.

Given that they had, apparently, gone through Door #2, it was no surprise that things would play out first and foremost through sex.

Half an hour later— They'd given it half an hour! Of all that had happened, why did this warrant not only airtime, but a full half-hour of airtime? Ah. Of course. Because it was about sex. He sighed yet again. The coverage wasn't about the unspeakable horrors suffered by the boys. Not really. It was simply camouflaged porn. As were, and had been, so many crime dramas, especially that one called "Special Victims Unit" or some such. Such a clever series: it got porn onto prime time by pretending to shine a spotlight on the prevalence of rape-and-murder. But really, it was just a show about women being raped and murdered. Call it a crime drama, legitimize it that way, and you get to show women being raped and murdered. Yay!

If the network was *serious* about shining a spotlight on the prevalence of rape-and-murder, it would broadcast an hour-long documentary about it every night. Featuring women who were not airbrushed, women who were not so pretty, not so sexy, women whose bodies were not so artfully arranged. As it was, rape-and-murder was being presented in the context of entertainment. That said everything.

Marcus reached for his laptop. Time to get out his pornography unit for the IntroGen class. They'd have to discuss this new development. And they'd need background, context. To see that it really wasn't new at all.

He still remembered first preparing the unit. He'd been appalled, disgusted, horrified at what he'd discovered. He hadn't known.

And because of that, he'd also been ashamed. Beth had known.

He'd discovered that 80% of all porn explicitly degraded the woman. Humiliated her. In addition to physically hurting her. Which was done in 90% of it. It was alarming to realize that men—and not just a few of them, but *most of them* (the stats ranged from 60% to 80%)—saw these images, watched these images, *actively sought* these images, *enjoyed watching* these images *on a regular basis.*

And then wanted their sexual partners to do—did they really not know that the actresses were *acting?* Just *pretending* to like it? Did they really think the moans of pleasure were *real?* Well, he thought, apparently people approached the 'doctors' from *Grey's Anatomy* all the time for medical advice.

Marcus backed up. He'd been imagining men, but the average age of first exposure to porn was 11. Apparently boys as young as 8 watch porn. In fact, one study discovered that a whopping 90% of boys aged 8 to 16 watch porn online; another found that 30% of boys aged 9 to 16 watch it *every day.* As a commenter on Feminist Current pointed out, attributing the insight to Gail Dines, "These boys ... have likely never had sex with a female, and therefore there's no context for what they're seeing on their computer screens. Once they actually do begin having sexual experiences with young women, imagine how that will play out, after having watched women be brutalized or choked or degraded online for years prior." Indeed. Imagine. Except we don't have to imagine, Marcus thought. It's already happening. *Was* already happening, he corrected.

Given the large percentage of children, boys, watching porn, it might not have been surprising to discover that 20% of all internet pornography involved children. If it had been twelve-year-olds 'doing' twelve-year-olds. But, of course (of course?), it was adult men 'doing' twelve-year-olds. *Torturing* twelve-year-olds. Torturing *children*. There was no other way to say it. No other way one *should* say it. In *Big Porn Inc.*, the authors report seeing a video in which an infant girl about two years old is being held down by at least two men while she is being fully penetrated. During an interview, the man who had penetrated her said something like, "There's nothing like hearing that *crack* ..." He was referring to was the breaking of her pelvic bone.

One teenage boy told researchers, "A lot of what I know about sex is because of porn." Another said, "Growing up, watching porn—that's sort of where you get your grasp of what's normal and what's not."

And that's when it hit him: sick had become the new normal.

So that's exactly what he wrote on the board a couple days later for his IntroGen class: SICK IS THE NEW NORMAL.

Ethan and Devon had read the materials he'd made available online before the class, but so had five other young men who showed up that Thursday night.

"Devon told us about your class ..."

"We've been trying to enrol, but ..."

"Come in, yes, welcome!" Marcus gestured happily to some empty desks. "I imagine the Registrar's office is still in disarray, but don't worry about that, I'll make sure you get credit for your work. Do you have access to the material we've already covered? Have you been able to catch up?"

They quickly sorted out a few logistics, and then focussed on the evening's topic.

"So," Marcus gestured to the blackboard. "How did that happen? *When* did that happen?"

"Maybe the answer to the first question is in the answer to the second," Ethan offered.

"Explain," Marcus encouraged.

"Well, I'm thinking maybe it happened when the internet became easily accessible. And maybe that's also how it happened. It's just so easy to see it. Porn. You don't even have to look for it really. Just type in 'porn', hit 'enter', and there it is."

"Hypothesis #1," Marcus nodded.

"But that doesn't explain why so many men *choose* to type in 'porn'," Devon said, "and hit 'enter'. Again and again. I mean, curiosity could explain the first time. But then?"

"It's addictive," Leroy, one of the new students, suggested.

"Hypothesis #2," Marcus said. "So unless people know how addiction works, unless they use their willpower right at the start to say 'No', they'll get hooked, reeled in …"

"We don't use pornography," Jason, one of the other new students, said, with … bitterness in his voice. "Pornography uses us. To make its millions."

A few of the young men nodded.

"But," Marcus added, "let's not lose sight of the fact that porn isn't some inert substance like alcohol or heroin. It's the assault, subjugation, and humiliation of real, live people that men become addicted to."

"I'm a little uncomfortable with calling it addiction," Ethan spoke up. "I mean, doesn't that absolve men? If it's a disease, something they aren't responsible for, something they can't control—"

"First," Leroy responded, "I don't think calling it an addiction necessarily means it's a disease. And second, a lot of people, strong people, do beat their addictions."

"So most men aren't as strong as they like to think," Ethan said. No surprise.

Devon nodded. "And they can't have it both ways."

"Explain."

"Well," Devon turned to Marcus, "whether it's an addiction or not, and whether it's biochemical or sociocultural, like we discussed last class, either their violence *is* within their control, they *have* agency, free will, whatever, in which case they're just weak-willed, not strong enough to resist, not as strong as they like to think," he nodded to Ethan, "and they should be locked up for criminal behaviour, or it's *not* within their control, they *can't help themselves*— in which case, again, they should be locked up. Because they're a danger to society."

"At a minimum, if they can't control themselves, they shouldn't be allowed to hold any position of power," Ethan suggested.

"But," protested Jason, "we don't have enough prisons to lock up, what, half of the male population?"

"*Over* half," corrected Daniel, yet another one of the new students, nodding to the material on his desk. "So we need another solution. And if it *is* a biochemical problem, we should be looking for a biochemical solution."

"Castration?" Ethan asked.

"Whatever inhibits or reduces their testosterone."

"A burdizzo," suggested Jason.

They all turned to him.

"I read about it on Feminist Current. They use it on baby livestock. Male baby livestock. It's a clamp that collapses the blood vessel leading to the testicles. Doesn't hurt. But without blood, the testicles don't develop. Once the animals hit puberty, they remain, quote, 'calm, sweet-tempered, easy to get along with' unquote. They don't fight each other. And they still grow up to be, again quote, 'big, beautiful, healthy animals,' unquote."

"Sounds good to me," Ethan finally said, seemingly speaking for everyone present. "Because asking—*begging* them to stop sure as hell hasn't worked."

"Still, why do we, why do men, gravitate toward the hardcore stuff?" Devon asked an hour later. It was disturbing. The stuff that was in the packet of materials he'd gone through the night before was, at least for him, an eye-opener. To say the least. Bottom line was most men enjoy porn, and most porn humiliates and/or hurts women. Which had to mean that most men enjoy humiliating and hurting women. Or, at the very least, watching other men humiliate and hurt women.

"Google."

"Explain," Marcus encouraged again.

"After a broad relevance match," Ethan said, "doesn't Google rank hits according to popularity?"

Marcus nodded. Google was nothing if not democratic. He'd often thought that that was a problem. And not just with Google.

"So at first," Ethan continued, "a hardcore porn site might make the top ten, it'd be *one* of the first page results, but soon—if Leroy's right about addiction—we know that when you're addicted, you need more and stronger to satisfy, your threshold goes up, right?—so soon the first page would be *full* of hardcore sites."

"And the second page and the third page," Leroy offered. "You might have to scroll through ten pages to get to a softcore site."

"Another thing—" Daniel hesitated, then continued, "and you all might think this is crazy—but I read somewhere that because of the growth hormones in our food, in meat and dairy products, people are becoming sexualized at an earlier age."

Marcus nodded. "We touched upon something similar in our last class. The possible connection between those growth hormones and testosterone levels." But they hadn't taken it to mean an earlier puberty. It was an interesting possibility.

"Okay," Marcus summarized, "Ethan and—Hiroshi, is it?—I want you two to investigate Hypothesis #1. Is the rise in porn use due to the rise in internet access? Perhaps you can at least establish correlation. Does the timing fit? But secondary research only," he emphasized. He wanted them safe in their rooms or in the library.

"Leroy and Devon, you're on Hypothesis #2. *Is* porn addictive? If so, *how* so? Or *why* so?

"Daniel, Jason, and—I'm sorry, I've forgotten your name already—"

"Adesh."

"The three of you are on Hypothesis #3. *Is* puberty starting earlier these days? Is there an increase in testosterone across the board? And is there a link to what we're eating?"

"And what hypothesis are *you* going to investigate?" Devon smiled at Marcus.

"Well, I think men have *always* been violent," Marcus said. "I don't think the need for violence, or even cruelty, is new. There's always been war. And look at the Inquisition.

"On a more personal note, I remember my grandfather watching 'the fights' on TV. 'Hit him! Hit him again!' he'd shout, punching the air. And he didn't even know the guy he was urging to be hit. I was horrified. My own grandfather was happily, enthusiastically, encouraging some stranger to be hit, to be *hurt*.

"I also remember being in a movie theatre watching *Rollerball*.

The original one, back in the 70s, not the remake. And just as James Caan's character raised his spiked fist above the face of the other guy who was down, people in the audience started cheering him on. 'Smash his face!' 'Yes! Do it!' It was actually quite … frightening. There I was surrounded by a crowd, a mass, that was being worked into a violent frenzy—"

"What did you do?"

"I left. I got up and left the theatre as quickly as I could. Careful not to break into a run."

A few of the young men nodded at that instinct. The rabbit that breaks into a run is the one that's caught. Killed.

"Okay," Adesh spoke up, "but how does this innate tendency to violence you're suggesting we have—how does that translate into this?" He lifted the porn packet. He preferred to annotate with pen, so like Daniel, he had printed out the materials.

"That is the question, isn't it. One hypothesis is that in the past, the code of chivalry protected women and children from men's violence, but with the rise of feminism, with the advocacy of equality, that code has disappeared: if there's equality, there's no need for male protection. And so now women and children are just as much a target as men have always been. Hypothesis #4."

Several of them were nodding their heads. No doubt every one of them had been a target at some point in their lives.

"Hating women isn't new," Marcus continued. "Insulting women has a long history. At least since the 1950s, coaches have been calling their losing team 'ladies' with such derision—"

"'You throw like a girl!'"

"'Don't be such a pussy!'"

"'Get out of my way, bitch!'"

"I dunno …" Adesh wasn't buying it. "I'm not sure chivalry ever protected women. Consider the Salem witch trials. And it used to be legal for a husband to hit and rape his wife."

"And even if that hypothesis is correct," Daniel looked at Adesh, then at Marcus, "even if feminism *has* destroyed the code of chivalry, why aren't men just beating them up more? I can't believe I just said 'just'," he added, apologetically, "but what I mean is why is the violence *sexual?*"

Marcus nodded. He'd thought about that. The prevailing theory was that pornography sexualized violence. Watch enough of it and you start to become sexually aroused by violence. But maybe violence already sexual. It was already exciting, certainly. Arousing, even. But— And— Was it also the other way around?

"Bouncer wisdom is 'They're either gonna fuck or fight'," he said. "Maybe the male aggressive impulse is that close, that indistinguishable, from the male sexual impulse. Maybe for men, sex *is* violence. Hypothesis #4b."

"So ... we're wired wrong?" Hiroshi wondered aloud. In the silence that had followed Marcus' suggestion.

"And porn has capitalized on our faulty wiring, and the increased hormones have exacerbated it," Marcus summarized.

"What's happening now does seem to support that bouncer wisdom," Devon observed. "Men can't fuck anymore, because the women are gone, so they *are* fighting more."

"Except that men *can* still fuck," Ethan said quietly, tilting his head to the 'pretty boy trade' materials on Daniel's desk. "They're making sure of it."

Marcus nodded as well, then led them in a slightly different direction.

"This may be a bit of an aside, but the name, what they're calling it, made me think of these." He opened a couple bookmarks on his laptop, and since he'd already connected it to the room's system, two images appeared on the large screen at the front of the room: Gainsborough's *The Blue Boy* and a cover of *Little Lord Fauntleroy*.

"I don't know if you're aware of the re-consideration of Western art that's going on," he continued, "but basically, we're thinking now that much of it is, was, porn."

He saw their eyebrows raise.

"Consider the tradition of the nude. Rubens, Gaugin, and so many, many others. Why would there be so many paintings of nude *women*? If they were truly just doing studies of the human body, wouldn't there be as many nudes of *men*? As many nudes of *old* human bodies?

"Excepting portraits of the nobility, almost every single female figure in the history of Western art is either nude or has a breast or at least a shoulder exposed. In some, the nudity is ridiculously incongruent. *Luncheon on the Grass*, for example." He quickly found and displayed the piece.

"There *are* some male nudes," Daniel spoke up. "Michelangelo's *David*, Donatello's *David*."

"And Michelangelo was gay," Ethan said, smiling. "Don't know about Donatello."

"So are you saying," Leroy ventured, "that the Gainsborough and Fauntleroy images are, like, 18th century child porn?"

Marcus nodded. "Just a thought. I haven't had a chance to follow it yet."

The young men considered the possibility.

"Given the emergent 'pretty boy trade'," Marcus continued after a moment, "porn's only part of it." He started uploading, sharing, some additional information. "The sex industry is the largest and most profitable industry in the world. In addition to porn, there's phone sex, strip clubs, street prostitution, brothels, mail order 'brides', human trafficking for sexual purposes, sex 'tourism' … Estimates indicate that as many as half of the four million people who are—were—will be—" he paused, in confusion, then dismay. "Half of the four million people trafficked each year were children, and two-thirds of those were at some point forced into the sex trade."

Marcus gave them a few minutes to skim through the new information he'd provided.

Finally Jason raised his hand, more a token gesture than anything. "The men who bought—who buy sex tour packages, who pay to have sexual access to a thirteen-year-old for one or two days—" The disgust was apparent in his voice. "Where do they think the children come from?"

"Good question," Marcus replied. "How deluded do you have to be? How blind have men made themselves?"

"And why?" Devon asked. "What *makes* a man so wilfully blind?"

"Buying sex is so pervasive," Marcus continued, "that one research team had a hard time finding men who *don't* do it. In order to have a control group, they finally had to change their definition of non-sex-buyers to mean men who hadn't been to a strip club more than twice in the past year and hadn't used porn more than once in the past month.

"Overall, they found that men who buy sex dehumanize and commodify women, view them with anger and contempt, lack empathy for their suffering, and relish their own ability to inflict pain and degradation. They were nearly eight times as likely as non-buyers to say they would rape a woman if they could get away with it. Asked why he bought sex," Marcus reported, "one man said he liked 'to beat women up'."

"And you're saying how many men buy sex?" Ethan asked quietly.

"Depending on the country, up to 90%. Though perhaps an accurate average is 30%. One in three."

He referred back to the factsheet he'd prepared.

"In the state of Georgia alone, 400 girls *a month* become—became—victims of the sex trade. 100 were used each night, by some of the 750,000 men in Georgia who used them."

He paused, then said, "One might ask why Georgia wasn't

declared a state of emergency until every single one of them was castrated."

"So no wonder," Devon said after a moment's silence. The others waited. "I mean, with all this—" he gestured vaguely, then tried again. "Men see how women are treated in porn, they treat prostitutes the same way, and then it leaks out, crosses over, into our everyday attitudes, and our everyday actions, toward women."

"Or is it the other way around?" Leroy suggested. "We start with the hatred and subordination of women, and that leads to the porn and prostitution."

"Maybe it goes both ways," Daniel said. "Maybe it's a vicious circle, a self-reinforcing feedback loop, that just gets bigger and stronger ..."

"But why do men hate women so much?" Devon asked. "That's the part I don't get. I mean, even when they're not even here, they hate them."

"Maybe they don't hate women. Or not *just* women," Daniel suggested. "Hypothesis #5. Maybe we just need to hate *someone*. Women, homosexuals, blacks, browns, yellows ..."

"But *why?* Is our need to hate so great, we'll hate anything? For no reason whatsoever?" Devon looked at the others helplessly. "I mean, are we— Are we also hardwired to hate? In addition to being hardwired to hurt?"

And yet, Marcus thought that evening, there isn't an entire subculture—*subculture?*—of, for example, whites hating, and hurting, blacks. Of black-skinned men being whipped by white-skinned men—and smiling about it. Just to make sure, he decided to google— There wasn't even a word for it.

29

James died while Andrew was having a cup of coffee.

Kyle had gotten a job, security guard at the mall, for which he was hired after a one-week intensive course of training. Andrew had urged him to get a different job because he was afraid Kyle would get hurt and then what?

But, he had to agree, it was the quickest and easiest option. There weren't a lot of evening jobs available, unless he wanted to become a maid or a waitress—interesting how some places insisted on still calling them that. Was it to justify the undoubtedly low wages?

So they divided the household work by rooms. One week Andrew did 'kitchen' which included buying food, making meals, and keeping the kitchen clean, and the next week he did 'bathroom and living room' which included keeping both clean and tidy.

They each kept their own room clean—Timmy and Tommy now slept in and shared Andrew's room, and Kyle and Evan got the boys' room. No one was happy about that. But then, no one had been happy since before the women had disappeared.

They each did their own laundry.

And they each did their own errands—banking, shopping … Andrew suddenly realized one day that they wouldn't have any more books by Julia Donaldson. Both of his boys loved *The Gruffalo*.

Their division of labour, while fair, meant that neither of them had much time to relax. Eight hours of work at work was followed, every day, by another two or three hours of work at home. Weekends were a little better, but …

Andrew was surprised to discover that Kyle had had a daughter as well. So Evan had lost his mom *and* his sister. He withdrew. He acted out. Andrew got used to hearing "You're not my Dad!" And he watched carefully to make sure Evan didn't vent his feelings on Timmy or Tommy.

Speaking of which, Timmy still cried himself to sleep almost every night, sobbing for "Mommy"—which didn't help the situation. And Tommy had started throwing tantrums on a daily basis; he'd somehow gotten it into his head that it was Daddy's fault James was gone. Both of them became inseparable from the huge stuffed gorillas he and Diane had bought for them the previous summer.

He and Kyle thought about hiring a third partner, to do all the household stuff, all the kidcare stuff, and all the errands, but they couldn't afford to pay such a person what they should.

They finally agreed that they would give each other Saturday or Sunday off. It was wonderful, Andrew thought, his first Sunday off. He had twenty-four hours to himself. He could go anywhere, without having to take Timmy and Tommy with him; he could do anything, without having to limit himself to what he could do with Timmy and Tommy in tow. A whole twenty-four hours. That hadn't happened since the women had disappeared.

Kyle missed his wife, Kerri. Andrew often saw him looking at the photos he had on his laptop, touching the screen tenderly, tears in his eyes. And at the beginning, he could tell himself that Christine was safe with her mom, wherever that was. He just needed to hold on. Everything would be okay. But as time passed, he, like most men, started to believe, started to accept, that the loss was permanent. He was never going to see Kerri or Christine again.

It had been Andrew's weekly cup of coffee. His Saturday or Sunday cup of coffee. That was all he could afford. One cup of coffee a week. Otherwise, he drank beer. Or water, from the tap. The city plumbing still worked, thank god, toilets included.

But otherwise? Food, unreliable. Clothing, mostly gone. Electronics, mostly gone. Transportation, unreliable. Sure, there were lots of mechanics available. It was the parts that were not. Business in general, unreliable. Some had adapted and recovered their efficiency, but if they did so by paying their now-male receptionists, clerks, assistants, etc. what they deserved, they went bankrupt. Unless everyone else on the payroll took a pay cut. Which happened only in a very few cases. And if they paid their now-male receptionists, clerks, assistants, etc. what they had paid their female receptionists, clerks, assistants, etc., well, they probably *hadn't* recovered their efficiency. And in any case, they were probably still in trouble depending on what supplies they needed to carry out their business. So any business still in business was likely operating at significantly reduced volume. And as for education, health services, social services? All, in a word, pathetic.

And everywhere anger, frustration, grief, aggression, violence, injury, death.

Andrew and Kyle limped along, living day to day, trying to keep themselves and their kids alive. Uninjured. Not sick. It could take months, maybe years, for the hospitals to recover.

They stocked up on everything—food and first aid/pharmaceutical supplies mostly—when available.

They made do without ... a lot.

The media—internet, TV, radio—all of that was operational, more or less.

But since North America hadn't yet felt anywhere near most of the repercussions of what was happening in other countries, the worst was yet to come.

30

A week later, there was another news item about the pretty boy trade. Apparently parents—why didn't they say 'fathers'? they'd always said 'mothers'—were outraged. They were taking to the streets, demonstrating, storming City Hall, occupying every police precinct, demanding that a stop be put to the trade.

Marcus sighed.

Why hadn't outraged 'parents' stormed the courts and occupied the police precincts when it was *girls* and *women* being kidnapped and forced into the sex trade? Everybody had known about it. Certainly the millions of men who rented or bought female bodies for their sexual use had known about it. But apparently it wasn't important enough to make the daily news. Apparently it wasn't as important as men's sports, which were guaranteed a full ten minutes during every bloody broadcast. Marcus turned off the TV in disgust.

The phone rang.

One of the stations he'd contacted wanted to know if he was still interested in being interviewed.

Sure, what the hell.

He spent the morning organizing his notes, preparing interview questions—that's how it was these days: you weren't to expect your interviewer to have done any prep, to be informed about the issue, to have appropriate questions ready. Marcus wondered, not for the first time, whether, similarly, news anchors had always been nothing more than good readers, hired because they *looked* authoritative and could be trained to *sound* authoritative. He'd noticed that often their pauses weren't quite in the right place and their emphasis wasn't quite on the right words. At least not if their purpose was to help people understand. But of course that wasn't their purpose. The pauses and emphases were positioned to keep people paying attention, to keep them *trying* to understand. And to keep them thinking that there was actually something important coming up.

"Hello, Dr. Marcus Epherine, welcome to our show!" Chuck, the host, was cheerfully enthusiastic.

"Hello, thank you for inviting me," Marcus responded, with measured sobriety. Cheerful enthusiasm was inappropriate.

"Could you tell our listeners a bit about yourself?"

"Certainly. I teach Sociology and Gender Studies at the University—"

"You're not going to go all feminist on us, are you?" Chuck chuckled.

"Yes, I am," Marcus replied evenly. "Do you think women are inferior?"

"Well, when you put it that way—"

"How else would you put it? Isn't that what a feminist is? Someone who *doesn't* think women are inferior? Who doesn't think they should be subordinated—"

"We have a caller already, you're on the air—"

"Yeah, who is this knob? Tell him to grow a pair!"

What? Marcus ignored the comment. "In any case, I'm more against sexism, on both—"

"So what's your take on this disappearance act the women have pulled?"

This disappearance act? "Could you be a little more specific?" Marcus said coldly.

"What I mean is what do you think's going on?"

"Well, I don't have any theories about the actual disappearance, that's a problem for the physical scientists," Marcus said, realizing full well that his interviewer wouldn't know the difference between physical science and social science, "but my students recently did a study, a rather cursory study, of *men's reactions to* the women's disappearance, and the results are overwhelming clear. Most men are expressing anger and, at the same time, a sense of 'good riddance'. How do we explain that?"

"I don't see the problem."

Seriously? Marcus spelled it out. "If you're happy to see something gone, why would its disappearance also make you angry?"

"Ah. And *your* explanation is?"

"Well, I suspect most men need women, for all sorts of things, things they don't even recognize, or didn't recognize, but maybe are seeing now ... but they don't *want* to need them. Our society defines manhood as independence. So instead of getting angry at themselves for needing, they get angry at the thing that's needed. Women."

"And we have another caller, you're on the air—"

"Hey dude, they need us too!"

"For what?" Marcus asked the caller. "If we paid them what we pay ourselves, they *wouldn't* need us." Ah. Is *that* why equal pay for work of equal value had met such resistance? He'd been thinking it was because men didn't recognize, couldn't assess, value. But maybe it was because men *wanted* women to need them. Why? So they could feel important. But wouldn't you rather be *wanted?* Maybe men didn't think they *could* be wanted, just for themselves, so they went instead for being needed. And maybe that's why lesbians and single-by-choice women were such a threat. They were proof that women *didn't* need men. (*Or* want them.)

"That's not what I'm talking about," the man snickered. Then hung up.

"And we have another caller, you're on the air—"

"What I want to know is how is the species going to survive without women to—you know."

"'You know'?" Marcus raised his eyebrows. How old were these men?

"Yeah, you know!"

"You can't say it?" The man probably couldn't say 'menstruate' either. Or 'vagina'.

"Sure, I can say it, but—"

"But what?"

"You know!"

"No, I'm afraid I don't." He wanted the man to come to grips with sexual reproduction. Surely it was time.

"I think," Chuck came to his rescue, "our caller is concerned that there will be no more children. To carry on the species."

"After all that's happened ..." Marcus started to reply, then backed up. "We have no schools, we have no hospitals, our justice system is crippled, over a thousand, perhaps a hundred thousand, lines of research have had to be discontinued, we are in a state of social and economic collapse of a magnitude that has never been seen before—and you still see women as mere incubators?"

"And we have another caller, you're on the air—"

"Give 'em an inch," the caller chuckled with innuendo, "and they'll take a mile. Soon they'll be running things."

Marcus sighed. No matter how nuanced the issue, it was almost always reduced to 'male vs. female'. Either/or. And competition between the two. The measures of a simple mind. A lazy mind. On testosterone.

"Would that be so bad?"

"Man oh man are *you* pussy-whipped!" the caller laughed.

"Look, I asked a serious question," Marcus ignored the laughter. "Would that be so bad? If women were in positions of power and responsibility? I'd like to hear your answer."

But he'd hung up. Of course he had.

"Look, the problem is," Marcus tried again, "we're living in a world—we've *been* living in a world—divided by sex. Males on one side, females on the other. Then we assign, mostly in an arbitrary fashion, all sorts of attributes to one or the other side. Males are supposed to be strong, competent, powerful, assertive, and so on. Women are supposed to be sensitive, submissive, beautiful, and so on. But mostly they're supposed to be sexual. And then, to top it off, we say all the masculine stuff is better than all the feminine stuff.

"And if anyone dares cross the line between the two— If a man is sensitive, we make fun of him and beat him up. If a woman is competent, we insult her and beat her down.

"What the hell is wrong with us?" Marcus asked. "Wouldn't it be a *good* thing for men to be sensitive? To be *aware* of others? Wouldn't it be a *good* thing for women to be competent? Why are we so hell-bent on maintaining the sexist system?"

"I don't think it's as bad as all that," Chuck interjected.

"Oh no? Listen." Marcus pulled out a sheet of paper from the folder of notes he'd brought with him. "These are posts from a website called *Everyday Sexism*." He started to read them aloud.

> "I can't help but notice that when I insist that people working for me do their job on time and properly, I am an 'uppity bitch'. My male colleague who does the same thing is a 'natural leader who gets things done'."

"A few years ago I was going to buy *The Economist* at a magazine shop at the airport. The store clerk ... insisted that I'd grabbed the wrong magazine and told me he was concerned because I had no one to explain the articles to me ..."

Beth had told him about the site and as he'd read what was there, he'd become appalled. And ashamed. Again. Because again he'd had no idea. He read a few more entries over the air.

"A couple of days ago, I was waiting for the bus alone. Some boys a year younger than me drove slowly by, and rolled down the window to yell 'CUNT', and [then laughed and drove off]."

"Guy grabbed my hips and made like he was banging me from behind when I bent over slightly in Walmart to pick up eggs. He and his buddy laughed like it was funny."

"While waiting to be picked up from the bus station in the wee hours of the night, a man slowed his bike enough to say to me: 'Hey babe, wanna give me a blowjob?'"

"Cleaning up some things on the floor at work, a male worker walks by and says 'So I see you're on your knees. Have you been waiting for me?'"

Marcus looked up at the interviewer. "Since when are all women's bodies available to all men?" he asked pointedly. Chuck just sort of smiled. Marcus was confused. He continued.

> "When I was thirteen, I was sitting in my grade eight math class when suddenly a boy in my class came up to me and grabbed my breast before running back to his friends and high-fiving each other."

> "At an academic conference a couple of weeks ago, I was chatting with the chair of my panel about my research. He spent the first half of our conversation staring directly at my breasts."

Marcus looked up at the interviewer again. "There's another website called *Who Needs Feminism* that has the same sorts of posts, messages left by women about their day-to day experiences of sexism. To date, there are 325 *pages* of posts."

After half an hour of reading the posts, Marcus had had enough. How did the women go on? Experiencing this *every day*? Pretty much *all day*? How is it, he wondered, *they* weren't the ones opening fire with a semi-automatic in a classroom full of *men*?

No wonder they left. The wonder is why it took them so long. He marvelled at their persistence, their hope, that they could change men, that they could change society ...

"One more," Marcus said, still on the air.

> "When a brilliant, hard-working, young woman at Yale, one of the *top* universities in the world, was awarded the Warren Prize for the highest scholastic standing, and it was announced that over the years she had received thirty-six As, she was booed. *Booed.*"

Marcus stared at his interviewer, then turned back to the microphone.

"We're better than that," he begged. "Aren't we?"

One day, the women were gone.

It wasn't enough.

Not nearly enough.

References

Chapter 4

https://www.oct.ca/-
/media/PDF/Attracting%20Men%20To%20Teaching/EN/Men_
In_Teaching_e.pdf (re women outnumbering men teachers at high
school level)

https://www.insidehighered.com/news/2013/02/21/new-book-explains-
why-women-outpace-men-education (re girls doing better than boys
at school)

Chapter 7

http://www.catalyst.org/knowledge/womens-earnings-and-income

http://www.conferenceboard.ca/hcp/details/society/gender-income-
gap.aspx (re pay gap)

http://gender.stanford.edu/news/2014/why-does-john-get-stem-job-
rather-jennifer

http://www.cnn.com/2012/10/01/opinion/urry-women-science/

http://www.yalescientific.org/2013/02/john-vs-jennifer-a-battle-of-the-
sexes/

Virginia Valian, *Why So Slow?* (Fidell p127-8)

https://www.insidehighered.com/news/2018/03/21/study-finds-female-
college-graduates-newly-job-market-are-punished-having-good (re
identical resumes)

http://blogs.scientificamerican.com/unofficial-prognosis/study-shows-
gender-bias-in-science-is-real-heres-why-it-matters/ (re identical lab
reports)

http://link.springer.com/article/10.1007%2FBF00289673#page-1 (re
identical essays)

http://files.eric.ed.gov/fulltext/ED067585.pdf

D. W. Tresemer, *Fear of Success* (re John/Anne studies)

Dale Spender, *Man Made Language*

Robin Lakoff, *Language and the Woman's Place*

Linda Babcock and Sarah Laschever, *Women Don't Ask*

Chapter 8

http://www.macleans.ca/wp-
content/uploads/2014/09/MacBlog_Feminism.jpg

https://beingawomaninphilosophy.wordpress.com/

http://www.physicscentral.com/buzz/blog/index.cfm?postid=51120198
41346388353 (re GRE scores)

http://webs.purduecal.edu/philosophy/graduate-school-preparation/ (re
LSAT scores)

Marilyn Waring, *If Women Counted*

http://www.webcitation.org/6HU4a0KMl (re Marilyn Waring)

http://www.apa.org/topics/divorce/

Chapter 9

http://www.vocativ.com/culture/society/anita-sarkeesian-threats/

http://www.theguardian.com/technology/2015/aug/29/anita-
sarkeesian-gamergate-interview-jessica-valenti

Chapter 11

http://www.apa.org/action/resources/research-in-action/protect.aspx

http://www.eurekalert.org/pub_releases/2010-10/oup-wvt101510.php
     (re watching violence desensitizes …)

Chapter 13

http://www.salon.com/2015/03/04/no_means_yes_yes_means_anal_th
     is_new_film_will_change_how_you_think_about_rape_culture/

http://thesocietypages.org/socimages/2010/10/17/yale-frat-pledges-
     chant-no-means-yes-yes-means-anal/ (re 'no means yes')

http://practice.findlaw.com/human-resources/women-not-gaining-
     ground-in-big-law-firms-says-nawl-report.html (re women making
     partner less often)

https://www.washingtonpost.com/news/on-
     leadership/wp/2014/02/18/large-law-firms-are-failing-women-
     lawyers/ (re women leaving law)

Chapter 21

https://www.dosomething.org/facts/11-facts-about-sweatshops

http://www.playsweatshop.com/sweatshop.html

http://www.theguardian.com/commentisfree/2010/oct/14/apple-
     foxconn-china-workers

Chapter 26

http://www.techaddiction.ca/files/porn-addiction-statistics.jpg (re
     $3,000/second)

http://stoppornculture.org/about/about-the-issue/facts-and-figures-2/

http://list25.com/25-shocking-facts-about-porn/ (re "30 million
     …combined.")

http://www.covenanteyes.com/pornstats/

https://www.rutherford.org/publications_resources/john_whiteheads_c

ommentary/americas_dirty_little_secret_sex_trafficking_is_big_bu
siness

http://www.shessomebodysdaughter.com/get-the-facts-about-sex-
trafficking

Chapter 28

http://www.collectiveshout.org/the_sex_factor_mainstreaming_and_no
rmalising_the_abuse_and_exploitation_of_women

http://www.psychguides.com/guides/porn-addiction/

http://nobullying.com/what-is-porn-addiction-to-porn-its-symptoms-
treatments-and-the-myths/ (re violence in porn, etc.)

https://wsr.byu.edu/pornographystats

http://www.telegraph.co.uk/education/educationnews/8961010/Pornog
raphy-is-replacing-sex-education.html

http://www.business-standard.com/article/news-ians/watching-porn-
sexting-on-rise-among-canadian-teenagers-survey-
114060301350_1.html

http://www.feministcurrent.com/2015/10/05/will-treating-porn-as-a-
drug-addiction-help/

Gail Dines, *Pornland*, (re first exposure, age 11; re largest group, age 12-
17)

http://radicalhubarchives.wordpress.com/2012/03/11/big-porn-inc/

Melinda Tankard Reist and Abigail Bray, *Big Porn Inc: Exposing the Harms
of the Global Pornography Industry* (re hearing the crack)

http://mojuproject.com/about/human-trafficking/ (re human
trafficking)

http://www.catwinternational.org/content/images/article/212/attachme
nt.pdf

http://www.newsweek.com/growing-demand-prostitution-68493 (re Farley's research)

http://prostitution.procon.org/view.resource.php?resourceID=004119

https://www.mentalhelp.net/blogs/why-do-men-go-to-prostitutes/ (re depending on the country …)

http://thesoutheronline.com/frontpage/?p=8162 (re Georgia)

http://www.feministcurrent.com/2015/07/23/male-violence-is-the-worst-problem-in-the-world/

Chapter 29

www.everydaysexism.com

http://whoneedsfeminism.tumblr.com/

Christopher Buckley, *Wry Martinis* (for Warren Prize incident)